Dusk

ROBBIE ARNOTT

Dusk

ASTRA HOUSE ◭ NEW YORK

Astra House
A Division of Astra Publishing House
astrahouse.com

Printed in the United States of America

Library of Congress Cataloging-in-Publication Data

Names: Arnott, Robbie, 1989– author.
Title: Dusk / Robbie Arnott.
Description: First U.S. edition. | New York : Astra House, 2025. |
Summary: "In the distant highlands, a puma named Dusk is killing shepherds
and twins Iris and Floyd—out of work, money and friends—decide to join
the hunt in pursuit of the bounty"—Provided by publisher.
Identifiers: LCCN 2025005739 | ISBN 9781662603303 (hardcover) |
ISBN 9781662603310 (ebook)
Subjects: LCGFT: Novels.
Classification: LCC PR9619.4.A767 D87 2025 |
DDC 823/.92—dc23/eng/20250210
LC record available at https://lccn.loc.gov/2025005739

First U.S. edition, 2025
10 9 8 7 6 5 4 3 2 1

Design by Pan Macmillan Australia.
The text is set in Adobe Garamond Pro.
The titles are set in Adobe Garamond Pro.

The author and the publisher have made every effort to contact copyright
holders for material used in this book. Any person or organization that may
have been overlooked should contact the publisher.

Aboriginal and Torres Strait Islander people should be aware that this book
may contain images or names of people now deceased.

For Emily

Dusk

1

WORD REACHED THE twins that a puma was taking shepherds up in the highlands. And not just shepherds—the hunters who'd tried to catch the creature were being killed, too, killed and dragged through the snow and devoured. There was a bounty, apparently. A decent price. That's all the twins heard.

They'd never seen the highlands. Nor had they ever seen a puma—the species had been driven out of the coastal and lowland forests when they were only children. And they couldn't be sure the story was genuine. There was every chance it was rumor or exaggeration.

But they were low on money and out of work, with no leads to follow or offers before them. Winter was ending and jobs were around, but nobody they knew wanted to know them. So they chewed on the story of the puma for a few days, hoping something else would turn up. When it didn't, they bought supplies and extra blankets and turned their horses west, toward the clean light of the high plains.

They traveled up the northern passage, through the golden wattles while their last flowers still brightened the air. All that divine color might have felt like an omen: heaven leaking between the trees. But once they reached the plateau the truth of this country was revealed to them. A vast field of rock and tussock grass, tar black and wet brown, broken apart here and there by half-iced tarns and forests of small trees. The only shine in the land came from a few loaves of snow, soft wreckage scattered across the plain. In the distance, white peaks cut into a clear sky.

The female twin was in the lead. At the crest of the trail she had a minute to take all that lonely country in, feel the sight of it drift and settle through her. She stared longer than she normally would, and barely noticed when her brother reached her side. Where her eyes had gone wide, roaming across the broader contours of the land, his tracked small, scanning its intimate features.

She pulled at the collar of her coat. "Cold."

Breath fogged from his mouth. "I suppose."

"Different, though."

"Different enough."

He pushed his heels into his horse's flank. It began

picking its way over the trail, carrying him off the plateau's hard lip. His sister followed, trying to study the rocks and trees the way her brother had, before letting her gaze rest on his back. It was subtly twisted; you could only tell if you knew where to look. A spine that pushed left from the tailbone and swerved right at the lungs. One hip that rode higher than the other. Shoulders that sloped unevenly away from a thick, tanned neck.

She knew her brother's back as well as her own. Knew how its snaking shape forced it to work against itself, sucking ache into his flesh. Knew how the cold tightened its kinks.

But if his back was troubling him he showed no sign of it. He sat straight, riding easy over the rough terrain, and she felt her body relax in response. Felt herself lean back in the saddle and let this strange high world hold her steady. And as her tension drained away she began to see the land properly. Saw the movement in it. Saw that they were not alone.

First she spotted the birds. Pulses of feathered texture in the nearest stand of trees: silvereyes, gray wrens, flame-chested robins. Clawed onto the upper branches was a gang of black cockatoos, ripping seed cones apart with the curved blades of their beaks, their yellow tail feathers flashing with the work. High above them all floated a pair of eagles, dark as death, arcing serenely through the weak clouds.

She wondered how she'd missed all this life, if her eyes were going, if she was losing her touch. Then she began to make out the furred heads of long-limbed hares, poking above the tussocks, watching the horses with careful patience. Beyond them a lone kangaroo, gray and calm.

And then, far across the plains: a herd of deer. Moving softly, light as lambs. Half-real and ghostlike in the thinness of the air. Stopping to stare at the twins before dancing away over rock, over snow, out of sight.

Their names were Iris and Floyd Renshaw, and they were thirty-seven years old. Both were short, but not notably so, and both had thick black hair and rough tanned faces, the kind of hair and faces—stiff, weathered, dried out—common in people who lived near heavy, salted winds, although it was not widely known where they were from. Little was known about them at all, except for the work they did, and even that was debated. Depending on who you asked, they were laborers, hunters, thieves or worse. Or just travelers. There was always somewhere they were traveling through and never anywhere they stayed long.

*

They spent the day moving across the plateau and into the highlands proper. They saw no fences, found no structures, met no other people. If they crossed any borders, they didn't notice them.

Iris had heard this country described as harsh, desolate. And while in all this sharp rock and wide sky she could see where those words might come from, she found no truth to them. Instead of harshness or bleakness she felt a freeing, lung-emptying openness that bounced off the hard stone, that waved through the thick mounds of tufted grass, threaded through the gnarled trees, fell down the chalky textures of the small tors she and Floyd rode below. That lived most of all in the tarns that appeared without warning, rising through the rock, pooling in her peripheries, dark and glossy and mirror-like. The sight of one made her pause, each new body of water a strange delight. She felt she could walk into them, despite the bite in the air, despite the snow gathered at their edges, and be received by the water with an impossible mineral warmth.

When the twins pushed through a tight clutch of trees they came upon something that promised more than a tarn. A lake: vast, metallic, untouched by wind or waves. Bordered on its northern edge by the rocky plain they'd been traveling over, but ringed on the west and south by low, snowy peaks, the same peaks they'd seen from the plateau's edge that morning.

Iris looked at Floyd. Looked for something that might

indicate he was experiencing what she was. But his face was expressionless. Eyes weary. Lips tight. Back both straight and kinked, if you paid attention. If you knew where to look.

They skirted the lake's shore—a beach of quartz sand, bright and coarse, closer to pink than to white—as the sun began cutting into the mountains that framed the water. As it fell further the light climbed over the peaks, giving the range an outline of radiant yellow, before dimming and dying and leaving the twins with only weak twilight to guide them until, on the far edge of the lake, they saw the blink of lanterns or fire.

As they came closer it was revealed that the blinking lights belonged to a tavern. Iris sensed Floyd's body tilt forward in his saddle. She had been looking for somewhere to camp, had imagined them rising from their tents to breathe fog at the lake the following morning, greeted by nobody, disturbed by nothing. But there was no denying a tavern's comfort would be welcome.

Behind them the lake reflected the fullness of the rising moon. And between the light of the moon and the shine of its reflection, Iris noticed something unusual about the building: it was surrounded by what looked like dead trees, limbless and leafless, bleached by age or death. They leaned over the roof, reaching toward each other in symmetrical, yearning arcs. Stark, pockmarked, more like ivory than wood. The ghosts of trees, or structures of priceless alabaster, or something else—an alien and unknowable grove that climbed into the night, beckoning the twins with a cold energy at odds with the tavern's warmth.

They tethered their horses in the small stable, unsaddled them, brushed them down, gave them each a blanket, held handfuls of oats to their mouths, threw hay into their stalls, filled their troughs with water, patted their noses, scratched and stroked the thinly furred tissue of their ears, leaned into the huff of their breath to whisper wordless love. Then they straightened their coats and hats and went inside.

Through a heavy wooden door they entered a wooden lobby: brass hooks nailed into polished wooden walls, scuffed wooden floorboards warped by use, faded paintings held by wooden frames, a wooden staircase leading to a darkened upper story. A side door opened, letting in raucous human sounds—clinking glasses, clashing voices—and a short, mustachioed man came through it, nodding at them before muting the noise by closing the door and moving to stand behind a wooden bench covered by a runner of green velvet.

He appraised the twins. Chose to smile. "Welcome to the Little Rest."

Iris rested a hand on the velvet and felt her fingers part the plush fibers: a foreign luxury after days out in hard air.

Beside her, Floyd fished in a pocket. He eyed the stairs. "One room. Two beds. One night."

The man's smile held. "Easily done." He named a price.

Floyd counted out some money and pushed the coins into the velvet before accepting a key the man handed him.

"Room five. Washroom is at the end of the upper hallway."

Iris couldn't tell if the comment implied anything; the man's voice was too neutral, his face too impassive.

Floyd wasn't concerned either way. He began moving to the stairs, but stopped when he noticed Iris wasn't following him. She was looking at the door the mustachioed man had come through, feeling the pull of all it promised: a room full of people and talk and stories that were foreign to her, that had nothing to do with her, that she could experience alone, unknown, Floydless.

Iris touched her pocket, searching for the hard shape of coins. "You head up. I'll see what I can learn from the locals."

Floyd grunted and kept going, taking the stairs slowly.

Iris lifted her hand from the velvet and made for the door.

She entered a low-ceilinged room, lit by the flick of

small candles and a fire glowing in a stone hearth. Smoke stained the light blue -gray. The walls held an array of antlers—Iris thought of the deer that had skipped away from them earlier in the day—and more dusty paintings. A bar ran the length of the room, where men were drinking something black and viscous from chipped glasses. Another group was standing by the fire in a circle, facing each other, looking serious but saying nothing.

Iris sat down. She watched the circle of men watch each other until the mustachioed man followed her through the door, eased himself behind the bar, cleared his throat and asked what she'd like to drink.

Iris looked at the dark liquid in the glasses of the other drinkers, the inky stains on their lips. The mustachioed man followed her gaze. "Peat wine. Made locally."

"Well." She pulled out some coins. "If it's local."

As he glugged her drink into a smudged glass a sonorous rumbling began to emanate from the circle of men. One of them had stepped forward, raised his drink—unlike the men at the bar, he and his fellow companions were drinking from pewter tankards—and started to hum a single deep note. When his breath ran out the other men took up where he'd left off, mimicking and amplifying the noise he'd made, and he began to sing. Simple and rhythmic, slow and sure—more of a tuneful chant than a melody. From the lyrics Iris could make out it was about a journey, or a woman, or maybe a friend (in the last cases, the woman or friend was clearly dead). At the end of each line the men surrounding him would echo his words in a calibrated mix of baritone and tenor.

When the singer was finished he returned to his place in the circle. Silence carved through the room. Then the man to his left moved into the center to lead his own song and the system repeated, a different tune but with a similar sentiment, delivered in the same call-and-response style.

Their voices filtered through Iris, sinking into her flesh rather than entering her ears. She drank. The peat wine was savory, foreign, rich with the taste of smoke and salt and iron and the burn of rough booze. Its syrupy consistency coated her tongue and throat. Her pulse slowed, her face heated, and the buzz the choir was sending through her blood grew louder. And perhaps it was this mixture of wine and song; perhaps it was the hours spent in the company of cold mountains and still water; perhaps it was her lingering awareness of the ghostly grove surrounding the tavern; perhaps it was because she was momentarily free of Floyd, while knowing he was safe; perhaps it was fatigue at the end of a hard day; perhaps it was all of it combined that made Iris lean back on her stool and feel a thin but taut connection to these things that were new to her, that were bright and strange, that she did not understand.

*

"They're preparing for the hunt."

The voice came to Iris as the second song ended. She looked to her left. The man sitting there had a short beard and shoulder-length hair, and was wearing a flannel overcoat. He was drinking peat wine and hadn't taken his eyes off the choir.

Immediately Iris felt the heat of him. Felt it in the moving of her skin. She shifted a shoulder, opening herself to the stranger. "I take it they're going to kill the man-killer."

"Going to try."

"You don't like their chances?"

He half-turned to her. "First time up here?"

Iris sipped her drink. She felt annoyed at being so easily identified, then felt the wine smooth it out of her. She gave him the slightest of nods.

He smiled, but softly, not gloating. "How's it suiting you?"

She thought of her day, of all she'd seen and touched and moved through, everything that had rattled around within her. But all of these things muddled her up, and she couldn't describe any of it. Her thoughts ran unbidden over other places she'd known. The sealing stations of the coast, foul-smelling and brutal, thick with casual violence. The rough mills of the rainforests, where the light was broken by thick canopies, where blue-black crayfish were snatched from dark creeks, where sawdust met damp air and stuck in her throat. The dairy farms of the southern valleys, where she and Floyd had found work slaughtering bobby calves with sledgehammers. The vast estuaries to the east, where they had thrown weighted nets into ink-dark currents, dragging out schools of flapping bream. The lagoons and wetlands, where they'd hunted black swans with barbed spears. The small islands off the coast, where the trees were beaten flat by the screaming winds they'd rowed through to join the muttonbird season, thrusting their hands down sandy burrows as likely to hold coiled snakes as thin-necked chicks. The sandstone quarries, full of miner's lung. The young towns, which bulged with crowds and smoke. All these places that frothed with the pace of the world, where life shook and strained, where one's blood ran fast. And it was only then, with these other places jumbling in her mind, that she found that she was able to focus on their journey through the highlands. She let the day play through her. Recalled their ascent up the golden-wattle path, across the cold plateau, beneath the lonely peaks, beside the death-still waters.

She blinked at the memories. Shifted in her seat. "It's not what I expected."

He took a drink. "It never is."

The third singer stepped forward and another song began, this one louder than the previous two, more bull-ish, more rousing. Iris and the bearded man turned back to the music, listening to the final note.

When the room again went quiet, he put his glass

down and leaned toward her. "These songs are from a time when a man was taken for every cat shot. I suppose they're reminding themselves of the danger, or exhorting each other to deeds of greatness. The usual stuff."

Iris let this comment sit, let another song run to its end. When she finished her drink she signaled for another before speaking. "No puma left where I'm from."

"There aren't many left up here, either. Perhaps only one, if you believe people. The one with the bounty. Too smart to trap, too mean to die." Iris saw a shiver in his lip as he spoke the creature's name: "Dusk."

The sound of a throat being cleared came across the bar. The mustachioed man was hovering, filling Iris's glass with a question in his face. "Ma'am, will your companion require dinner? I can send it up to your room. The galley's closing in a few minutes."

Iris became hotly aware of the bearded man beside her, the care with which he was ignoring the inquiry. "If my brother wanted anything, he would've asked."

The mustachioed man inclined his head and put the cork back in the bottle.

Iris turned back to the choir. "All these men for a single cat?"

"The bounty that the graziers are offering is enough for all of them." The bearded man's face went flat. "Maybe they feel safer as group. Or believe there's strength in numbers."

Iris was about to ask more when the mustachioed man—who had lingered at the bar behind them—interrupted. "It won't matter either way."

Iris turned to him, annoyed. "So little faith."

The mustachioed man shrugged. "I'm sure they're strong. I'm sure they shoot straight. But a hunter ten times their quality has already been hired. You must have heard—the graziers brought him all the way from Patagonia. A famous tracker, this man. A legend in the Andes. When he arrived he said it would take him three days, a week at most." He rubbed a cloth around the inside of a glass. "That was over a month ago. Hasn't been seen since." He seemed pleased with himself for passing on this information, but when he noticed the heat of Iris's glare he put the cloth and glass down and moved away.

Iris watched him go. When she turned back, the bearded man had stood up. He was stretching his shoulders, and Iris was surprised to see that he was tall; men like this always seemed to her, at first, like they were within an inch of her height.

"Dusk has taken five men, to my knowledge," he said. "Six, if you count the Patagonian. No wonder these fellows aren't going it alone." He extended his hand to her. "Patrick Lees."

She let his hand hang for a moment, gave him a proper look. She found no game or trick in his face. A moment later she pushed out a palm. "Iris Renshaw."

As he took it—thick fingers, gentle grip, rough nubs of skin that corresponded with her own—he peered over the bar at the menu written on a dusty blackboard.

"You eating?"

She felt the invitation in the words. Felt the briny fire of the peat wine course through her. Felt around in her head for what she wanted.

"No, I'm spent." She drained her glass, stood up. "Evening."

He nodded. "Evening."

Iris began to leave, walking slowly, thinking of his big hands, his neat beard, the ease of his talk. The strength in the size of him. She stopped at the door when she thought of something else.

"What killed the trees?"

Patrick Lees was still studying the menu. She couldn't tell if he'd watched her walk to the door. "Trees?"

"The ones around the building."

"Oh." He frowned. "They aren't trees. They're bones. An ancient sea beast, or so they say. The Little Rest sits in its ribs."

She waited a moment. "A sea beast."

Another man in the choir stepped forward and the singing struck up again. Patrick Lees pointed a hand to the nearest window. Now that she was no longer close to him he had to raise his voice. "Apparently this plateau was once a seafloor. The mountains, underwater. Can't say

I believe it, but there are the bones. There's the sky. What do I know, in the scheme of it all? Everything was something else once."

Upstairs, Iris found the washroom. She threw water over her face, rubbed off the day's sweat and dirt and grime. She could smell smoke in her hair, but didn't have the energy to wash it out.

In their room she found Floyd lying face down, still clothed. He'd left a candle burning beside her bed. His eyes were closed, but from the shallow heft of his breaths she could tell he was awake. She sat down, picked at her stiff laces, pulled off her boots, peeled off her socks, untied her hair. She changed into long johns and a nightshirt, feeling a weariness in even those small tasks before she ripped back the blanket and collapsed onto the pillow.

But though she was drained in both body and mind, she did not fall asleep. She rolled against the itch of the woolen blanket. She looked out the window at the sharp light of the stars playing off the towering bones. She listened to the wet pain in her brother's breathing for as long as her body let her. Then she got up, grabbed a jar out of his bag and told him to move over.

Floyd pulled in a breath. He held himself tight and

wriggled left, his lower half fishtailing over the sheet, awkward, violent. A hoarse bark fell from his mouth.

Iris climbed onto his bed and knelt over his hamstrings. She pulled up his shirt and took out each arm, not hesitating when he flinched. She threw the shirt on the floor, unscrewed the lid of the jar, dipped in two fingers and retrieved a glob of waxy ointment that smelled of sheep. Then she began to knead it into the skin of Floyd's back, aiming for the site of his old injury. She worked softly at first, with the points of her fingers, but gradually harder, using the heels of her palms. He endured her, wincing into his pillow, occasionally groaning.

She continued to work at him, pushing and needling, on and on, through the longest hours of the night, her arms and wrists throbbing, her fingers numb, until his spasming flesh suddenly relaxed and released him and he slumped away from her. His breathing took on the heavy rhythm of sleep, and she rose from the bed to wipe her reeking, glistening hands on the dark grain of the wall.

2

It was the simplest kind of curse. No magic, nothing otherworldly. The easiest of damnations, a trap stretched open for a lifetime, a barbed gift delivered at birth. Nothing more than a name: Renshaw.

In the morning Floyd rose from his bed with sharp purpose, his movements swift, his body iron-strong. He pulled on his clothes and stared out the window, studying the ribs that loomed through a thick bank of morning mist, as if seeing them for the first time.

Iris fought the light for as long as she could, fought the greasy hem of her blanket, fought fatigue, gritted eyes, groggy resentment. Then she got up anyway and came down to meet Floyd in the lobby, where he was talking to the mustachioed man—prim, clean, as if he'd both slept for an age and never gone to bed—about breakfast.

By the time she reached Floyd's side the conversation was over. She followed him into a dining room on the other side of the hall to the bar she'd sat in the previous night. On the far wall a fire burned orange. Men were sitting at small tables, drinking tea, fondling small rolls of brown bread. Iris recognized some of them from the night before, although none were hunters from the choir. None Patrick Lees, either, although she told herself she wasn't looking for him, not in particular. Steam from their breakfast and mouths had fogged the windows. As she and Floyd sat down at an empty table, Iris considered rubbing the glass clean with her sleeve, but decided it was too early in the day to dirty her shirt.

A boy brought a plate of rolls and a pot of tea to their table. As they began eating, Iris told Floyd what she had learned the evening before. She kept in all the details about the peat wine, the hunter-singers and the bounty, but was careful to give Floyd the impression she had gathered this information from an array of people, not one man alone.

He chewed his roll, wiped his mouth. "So it's real. The bounty."

"Seems that way."

Floyd looked at the fire, at the weak shapes of the morning flames. "How many did you say this Dusk has taken?"

Iris pushed a flat knife into butter. "Five or six."

Floyd took this in, still chewing on his breakfast.

Iris watched him until she grew sick of it. "We can hunt."

"Sounds like this South American could, too. And I'm sure the others that were taken weren't novices." A clump of bread hung wetly in his cheek. "More likely it would hunt us."

She scraped the butter onto her roll, putting her wrist into the smearing of it. "Worth finding out more, surely."

"We don't even have a rifle."

"Hasn't slowed us down before."

Floyd swallowed. Gave a sigh. "Could go talk to one of these graziers, I guess. They might have other work on."

She lifted her eyes to his. "You're scared."

He thought for a moment, turning her words over. Then he smiled. "You're not."

Through the rest of the meal they said little, and Floyd did not mention how she'd helped him the night before. But when they'd entered the room he had made sure she sat closest to the fire, which he loaded with more wood. He poured her tea and passed her milk. When she ran out of butter, he fetched more. And when he saw her straining to look through the fogged windows, he rose to wipe away the condensation with his coat, giving her a clear view of the clouded morning, the muddled light on the lake, the breath-like mist grazing the water.

*

In the stables they encountered other guests preparing to leave. As Floyd fetched their horses Iris found a reason to stand near the oldest man there, a bent-backed traveler with thick, wiry eyebrows. She commented on the weather, threw a barb at the Little Rest's breakfast, and small-talked at him until he sighed and talked back.

Afterward she found Floyd outside the stable door, staring up.

"Nearest sheep station is west of here." She rubbed her horse's neck, climbed onto its back. "Grazier's named MacLaverty."

Floyd's eyes were on the cradle of bones. "Looks like a ribcage."

Iris mounted. "Imagine that." She trotted around the stable, where she found a narrow path that led west. Floyd followed, eyes still up.

She'd thought the ride would be similar to the previous day's: bright, harsh, revelatory. But the trail was more cultivated. In place of rock and ice and tussocks there was hard grass, trodden flat by heavy hooves. Where mud glinted through the greenery it was covered with planks of milled wood. Iris suspected the land around them was different, too, but every feature of it was hidden from them by the mist, which hung thicker and lingered longer than it did in the lowlands and on the coast.

The only thing revealed to them that morning was a small river whose course their trail seemed to be following.

Iris watched it flow. Usually running water made her uncomfortable, but the way this one moved slowly, its face steely and quietly purposeful, brought about in her a feeling of gentleness that began in her neck and dripped through her, down into her dangling boots.

As they rode, Iris found that she was coloring the land beyond the mist with the stories she'd heard the night before. Somewhere nearby a peat bog was surely being hacked apart, its soggy fibers soon to be smoked into wine. Pumas stalked the wet air; hunters bled into the clouds. Great caches of ancient bones blended into the whiteness.

Finally, in the early afternoon, the mist began to clear. First it lifted from the river, pushed away by whatever current of air or vapor the warming day pulled from the water's surface. Then it retreated steadily across the land, revealing deep green fields of grass, more orderly than the tussocks they'd seen the previous day. Trees with pale-patched trunks and dusty blue leaves rose tall and lonely from the grass, never in groups or forests. As the mist lost more of its shape they began to see small herds of sheep. White-gauzed, black-faced, escorted by distant shepherds who never saw the twins or always chose to ignore them. There were no hares, no kangaroos, no birds to be heard or seen.

As the sun's weak burn broke apart the last of the mist, they could see where each field ended: in small clustered forests that ran into sheer mountains, taller and harsher than the gentle peaks they'd seen the day before, cased in snow and ice that near their summits gave way to great gray blades of bare rock, ranging across the northern, southern and western horizons, walling Iris and Floyd into a valley from which the only escape was the way they'd come.

They ate as they rode, stopping only to let the horses drink. With no mist, there was no part of the landscape obscured from them. River, fields, distant trees, vast ranges: it was all ever present and inescapable. Iris's mind left the peat wine, the pumas and the fossils behind. Again she felt emptied by the land, although where the day before the rocky plains had instilled in her a great pulse of freedom, she now felt hemmed in and dwarfed by the massive mountains that framed their passing. But it was not a claustrophobic feeling; there was pleasure in moving through it all, as if she was slowly discovering the right way—or perhaps just her way—to move through an old world.

Around three o'clock Floyd whistled. Iris, her eyes on the space where peaks met the sky, turned to see him pointing down a lane that sprang off the path. A thin column of smoke rose from the direction it led. Again Iris became aware that she was missing the details her brother saw, and before she could stop herself she rolled her shoulders at him, stretched her neck, showed him how lightly she could sit a-saddle as she turned her horse's nose down the lane.

Not long later they saw a homestead: a two -storied sandstone house that lifted from the grass, handsome and foreign against the distant backdrop of ice and rock. It was cut off from the wider fields by neat wooden fences. High windows in its roof accessed small balconies designed for lookouts or riflemen.

The smoke they'd seen from the main path was coming from a fire to the side of the homestead. Iris and Floyd rode toward it, knowing from experience that they'd be more welcome there than at the front door. As they neared it they saw flames curling up a stack of white branches, arranged in a tent above handfuls of blazing bark.

A boy was watching the fire. His body was a frame of hard points, all ribs and knuckles. A large pot sat near his feet beside a rusted metal tripod.

He turned when he heard their horses, showing them the youth in his features.

Iris removed her hat. "Afternoon."

The boy stared at them.

Iris tried a smile. "Glad to see the back of that mist."

He crossed his arms.

After a few seconds she let her lips drop. "We're hoping to speak with the grazier."

The boy looked out at the fields, at the creamy flecks of sheep on the far grass. "Boss will be in soon. Your best bet is to wait here." A thought twitched across his face. He indicated the pot. "I'll put in a good word if you get this boiling."

Floyd swung out of his saddle. "Be happy to." He winked at the boy, tethered his horse to the fence and began moving the tripod over the fire. As he lifted the pot the boy became alive with a sudden sense of freedom. A grin cut his face open and he dashed off behind the house.

Iris dismounted. "Kid figured you out quick." She tied her horse beside Floyd's. "He probably won't even see the grazier."

Floyd shrugged. He hefted the pot onto the tripod's hook, spilling some water onto the flames, which sizzled up at him. He fiddled with the contraption, adjusting the height. When he was satisfied he poked some larger sticks onto the fire and sat down beside it, stretching out his legs. Iris came to his side, removed her gloves and held her hands to the warmth.

They leaned into it for some time, methodically feeding more sticks into the fire's heart each time the flames lowered. When the water began boiling Floyd kicked the burning wood apart and raised the tripod to sit higher.

The pot took on a rolling simmer and the steam that lifted from it dissipated in the cold air, and the sun's arc dipped into the high ranges, and soon a rider appeared in the nearest field, coming toward them.

When the figure reached the fence they vaulted off their horse, left it untied and came through the open gate, closing in on the fire, revealing themselves: a woman, a few years younger than they were. Walking stiff out of her saddle, a day outdoors evident in the tangle of her hair. A long coat that had been made for the shape of her body. Face red with snow burn.

She came to the coals, peered at the water, did not acknowledge the twins. She used a stick to hook the pot off the tripod and place it on the grass, before pulling from her pocket a small pouch, which she opened and upended, spilling a shower of black-brown mulch into the water. She bent down to stir it with the stick, watched it whirl, watched it steep. She fetched a metal mug from her bag, placed a neat little strainer over it and poured in the steaming tea. Then she turned her bright, tired face to Iris and Floyd.

"Something I can do for you?"

Iris bent her neck. "Evening, ma'am. Sorry to trouble you like this. It's just that we're here to inquire about the bounty."

The grazier had cupped both hands around her mug. "Inquire away."

"Well." Iris felt herself shifting about, felt Floyd's quietness beside her. "Does it stand?"

"It does, assuming nobody's claimed it." Now the grazier looked up at them from across the fire, through the steam of the tea and the glow of the coals. "Who are you, then, when you're at home?"

Iris dipped her head. "Iris Renshaw." She indicated to her left. "My brother, Floyd."

The grazier's face tightened, as if she was searching for a memory, a connection in her mind. "From the lowlands?"

Iris kept her voice flat, her expression neutral. "Thereabouts."

The grazier kept searching, her eyes flicking about. But soon she gave up and came around the fire toward them. "Harriet MacLaverty." She shook both their hands, looked them in the eyes, her grip warm from the heated mug. "You fancy your chances, then?"

Iris let her body relax. "I wouldn't say that. Wouldn't even say we're going after it, at this stage."

MacLaverty looked up at the range, to where the dipping sun was coloring the snow orange. "You hunted cats before?"

"No, ma'am. They've been wiped out where we're from. We thought they were gone for good. Guess the last of them fled up here."

MacLaverty lifted the pot, poured herself more tea. "They were here first, to speak the truth of it." She looked to the twins, then back at the pot, until they pulled out their waterskins, emptied them onto the ground and held them out for her to fill. When she had done so they raised them in thanks and drank deeply, letting the bitterness of the tea ride their tongues, letting the heat swim through them, listening to MacLaverty as she continued.

"My grandfather brought them here, the fool. He and the other graziers. I suppose they shouldn't have brought the deer before them, but after the men saw off the first people and built their houses they looked around and realized they missed where they'd come from. As if they didn't know it'd be different." She shook her head. "The deer were meant to keep to the forests, waiting to be run down and shot. But they preferred the grass my grandfather planted. Who'd have thought? Multiplied like rabbits, bullied the merinos off the land. He and his colleagues tried culling them, but they couldn't shoot them through the mist, couldn't chase them over rock. So in their desperation they convinced each other that a mad idea was a good one, and five breeding pairs of puma were brought from the Andes, at great cost, to hunt the deer." Savage humor swam into her eyes. "They took one glance at our sheep and tucked straight in, stopping only to breed. Killed hundreds, cost us thousands. Didn't even look at the deer or the native creatures. Over the last decade we've managed to dwindle their numbers, drive them into the peaks." She took a long sip of tea. "But this one. This Dusk. They say she's the last of them." A strange lilt came into her voice. "Maybe we deserve all that she brings."

Iris let the evening fill the following minutes, waiting until the grazier moved to feed the fire to take up her questions again. "Can you tell us much about the beast? Its appearance, its range, its favored prey, where it was last seen?"

MacLaverty threw a log onto the coals. "She looks like every other puma. It's her personality that makes her dangerous." She nodded at the mountains. "Her range is up there, along with every other peak of the plains. Dusk hunts every station, all terrains, in all weather. She favors sheep, but will take anything. Especially anything that is stalking her." She pointed to a slight overlap in the mountains. "You'll get the most recent information about her in Rossdale. A day's ride from here, through the western pass. That's where everyone else after the bounty is. Where the tall fellow who came by earlier today was headed. Lees, I think his name was. Friend of yours?"

Iris felt the name in her throat, in her warming cheeks. But she stood still, shaking her head, taking care to appear unmoved. She hoped her brother bought it, before redirecting her line of questioning. "We heard about your famous hunter. This Patagonian."

MacLaverty cocked her neck. "Did you now?"

"Wondered if we'd heard right. That the puma took him."

She shrugged. "You've heard what I've heard. I never met the man. He treated with the other graziers, the ones who hired him. Horton and the rest. They tend not to consult me, not since my grandfather died. Although they were more than willing to accept my contribution to the bounty." She looked up at the range. A thin wedge of sun was all that remained of the day. "Can't be much hope for him by now."

A heavy silence followed.

Floyd turned to the darkening fields. "Any other work around?"

MacLaverty stretched her back. "There could be. I'd like there to be." Faint enthusiasm entered her voice. "Soil up here's fertile, full of tiny bones that look like fish or crabs. Makes no sense, I know, but grass just jumps out of it. If we could push the forest back, we could put more fields in. Get a few more head of sheep. It wouldn't be hard. But nobody will pick up an axe while Dusk is out there. No locals, anyway—they all knew at least one of the men she's taken. And even if they'd take the job—or if strangers like you would—I frankly wouldn't allow it. I'm not sending anyone else to their death. Can't have that hanging over my head.

"But if Dusk were gone, I'd start hiring in a heart-beat. I'd pay half wages in advance. And once the land is cleared, there'll be fences to build, more sheep to herd, shearing, upkeep . . . a whole life of work. Whoever kills the beast will have first pick of it all, I'd imagine, once they've spent the bounty. They'd never have to look hard for a coin up here. If they stick around."

Floyd nodded. His eyes were still on the fields.

MacLaverty yawned, stretched her back again. "Too late to head out again. You're welcome to camp here."

Again Iris inclined her head. "That's very kind." She would have said more, offered some kind of service in return, but she was distracted: she'd been thinking about Patrick Lees. How he hadn't told her he was going to hunt Dusk. How, if anything, he'd tried to give her the impression he was an impartial observer. Or maybe Iris had missed something he'd said. Maybe her mind had been muddled by the peat wine, by the choir, by how close he'd been sitting. How he'd smelled vaguely of turpentine and wood shavings.

MacLaverty waved a wrist. "I'm not going to turn a pair of travelers away at this time of day, am I? What fortune would that bring me?" She threw the detritus from her tea onto the grass. "Good luck to you both, whatever you choose to pursue."

She left them, going to her horse, leading it by the reins toward the stables.

Iris looked up at the wakening stars and used them to scrub her mind clean. Then she and Floyd untied their own horses and closed the gate behind them. They each cleared a spot on either side of the fire and unrolled their swags across the night-wet grass. They sharpened sticks with their belt knives and used them to impale smoked sausages that they retrieved from their saddlebags, which they heated over the flames, along with a tin of beans they wedged into the coals. When they'd eaten they loaded up the fire with a pyramid of logs and sat down before it, watching the flames climb over and into the wood.

The night deepened, revealing more stars, more gauzy textures in the distant blackness, the haze of galaxies. The air grew cold enough to needle their skin. As they shuffled closer to the fire they stuck to a convention they'd been following for years: that after the sun went down, they would not talk about anything that required a decision.

Instead they talked about what they'd seen that day. The weight and resistance of the mist. The treacle-like flow of the river. The twisted, ancient trees. The neat fields, the silent shepherds, the sudden surge of the mountains. The lack of birds. In soft voices they told each other about it all, passing the scenes back and forth like a pipe, building a shared world of memory.

Among all this talk of vision and experience, they mentioned only one piece of information. It came as they loaded up the fire for a final time and climbed into their swags.

"Sounds like there'll be plenty of work when this cat's

gone." Iris spoke across the embers. "Might even be able to stop moving about so much."

Floyd had curled his knees up to his stomach, his breathing steadying into sleep. "Might."

"A whole life of work. That's what she said." Iris rolled onto her back and drank in the cold field of stars. "A whole life."

3

A WHOLE LIFE earlier, when the twins were aged nine—
or perhaps ten; they could never get the seasons straight
in their heads—they were crouching on a beach, bleeding into the sand. Small, wiry, hungry. Hiding behind
a gray boulder brightened by a crown of orange lichen.
Not talking. Not breathing much. Tiny deep cuts on their
shoeless feet from the bladed shells they'd crept over to
reach this spot. Trickles of young life snaking from their
wounds to stain the white grains crimson.

Beyond the boulder eight skinless bodies lay on the
shore, their naked flesh dried a dark ruby by the salted
wind. Eyes and teeth lunged out of the stripped heads
in grotesque snarls. They were—or had been—fur seals,
heavy and meaty in death, robbed of the liquid grace that
had defined them in life. Their hides were drying on a
rack behind the beach, stretched out beside a set of long
rust-pocked knives that had been used to scrape away the

thick layers of fat between their muscle and skin, the fat that had warmed and cushioned them through their ever wet lives. This was now bubbling in a massive iron pot above a green-sparking driftwood fire, rendering down into oil, washing the coastline with a thick reek that made Iris and Floyd want to close their eyes and run away even more than the sight of the skinless seals.

Men were on the beach, too. Five of them sitting near the carcasses, drinking from brown bottles, watching the rush and retreat of the waves. A sixth man was stirring the pot of fat with a wooden pole, holding a dirty scrap of cotton across his mouth and nose with his other hand. Behind them, two women of the first people sat on the low dunes. Their eyes were closed and their necks bent back, their youthful faces and intricate shell necklaces pointing to the sky. The skin around their wrists was raw and red.

The twins watched the man stirring, watched the other sealers drink and talk, until a man and a woman staggered out from behind rocks further down the beach, singing and shouting, seemingly drunk. The sealers turned to the noise. The man began to swear at the woman; she threw a handful of sand into his face; he grabbed at her, missing at first but then tackling her to the ground. The sealers laughed, until the man started hammering his fists onto the woman's face and neck, and she began to scream. Then the sealers wearily stood up and wandered toward the brawling strangers. The stirrer went as well, which is when Iris and Floyd made their move, stepping silently out from behind the rock and dashing to the fire in a crouched sprint, pushing bloody toe prints into the sand.

When they reached the pot they were hit with the full horror of the smell—rotting offal, fishy death—and nearly retched. But they held shallow breaths, looked at each other, steadied themselves. They knew that they had no choice—that there was nothing else out there for them, beyond the beach or waves or anywhere, nowhere to go, no warm arms to fall into, no shelter in the world but each other.

Floyd grabbed one of the sealers' buckets. Iris snatched up a ladle, reached into the smoking cauldron, pushed through a skin of brown scum and began spooning out the boiling fat. Its bubbling surface spat viscous globs onto her skin; although she flinched, she didn't stop. It splashed further as she ladled, flying onto Floyd's arms. He wobbled and gasped but she kept spooning, and he held on.

As they worked they began to feel an intimate prickling on their skin. They looked up to see that the first women had taken their faces from the sky and were watching them, though neither one moved or called out. They just bored their eyes into the twins, a look both passive and powerful. Iris and Floyd stared, knowing they were communicating something but not sure what it was, before turning back to their hot thievery.

When the bucket was full and their wrists wore a patchwork of glistening burns, Iris tossed down the ladle and reached for the bucket's handle. Together they hefted the precious load and lurched into the maze of orange-lichened boulders that looked, from a distance, like they were on fire. Rendered seal fat slopped onto rock and sand and their still bleeding feet. By the time the sealers had lost interest in the brawling couple—when they'd kicked the wind out of his ribs and slapped the shout out of her mouth, and returned to their drinking—the twins had slipped away into the dunes, leaving a trail of spattered oil and bloody sand that the sealers never noticed, and that the first women never showed to them.

A few months later the twins were on their knees, their hands plunged into rich red soil, stealing again. It was early morning, and the world was silent and still but not cold: warmth climbed from the churned earth up into their fingers, up their arms, into their pigeon chests. Above them, muddled tints of blue and gold leaked into the eastern rim of the black sky.

They knelt side by side, thin sleeves rolled up, hands clawing through the soil. They were tired and wanted to rub at their eyes, but their hands were clagged with dirt, and they couldn't slow down: they had no choice but to work. When they found their prize—the dimpled orbs of potatoes—they pulled them out and dropped them into hessian sacks.

As the sacks filled the twins shuffled forward, pushing their hands into fresh patches of soil, following the shapes of the two adults in front of them, the man and the woman who'd brought them here, the same ones who'd staged the fight on the beach and made them take the seal oil: their parents. The work of digging consumed all four of them. There was no sound other than their scrabbling hands, their shuffling knees and panting breaths, until the morning was torn open by a dog's distant, furious bark.

Iris and Floyd reacted blearily, fearfully—not fast. Not like their mother and father, who were on their feet before the bark had faded from the air, grabbing their sacks and running for the dry forest at the edge of the field.

The dog barked again, sounding closer, and the twins stood up and began to follow their sprinting parents. After a few desperate strides Iris tripped on a furrow and fell, her haul of potatoes spilling and running away from her. Floyd heard her body smack the ground. Felt a sucking wrench at the thought of her in danger, in pain. He stopped, fell to her side, pulled her up, pushed her ahead of him as they ran, red flecks of soil flying up from their hard-skinned feet. They hit the tree line exhausted and filled with terror, with one sack of potatoes instead of two, and were greeted with rage and bitterness, with the hairy side of their father's hard hand.

They were at it again in a year's time. They were in an old silo, shin-deep in wheat. Early night, harshly dark, winter. Outside, the grassy paddocks they'd walked across were crusted with frost. Inside the silo, steam was rising from their skin as they worked to fill sacks with grain— the same hessian sacks they'd used to steal the potatoes, which in the intervening time they'd used as pillows and as blankets, and to wipe spilled rum off their parents' faces. When each was full of grain they heaved it through the tiny aperture they'd entered through. A full sack was heavy, and throwing one required both of the twins.

They worked through the darkness, shoveling with their hands, sweating into the wheat. They'd been told to be fast, that they could be discovered at any moment, that if they mucked around their parents wouldn't wait for them. So they filled the sacks at a savage pace, mindlessly, wanting only to be finished and free of the musty, creaking silo.

Half the sacks were full when they heard a hand slam three times on the outside of the wall. They began scrambling for the exit, dragging the empty sacks with them, knowing that leaving them behind would result in punishment. They skidded over the mounds of wheat, pausing only to drag each other up when they slipped. At the aperture they tumbled out and fell, missing the ladder, crashing into the iced grass. Frost bit into their cheeks, their necks. Pale pain on their skin. When Iris felt it she reached for Floyd's face, rubbing heat into him before she thought to warm herself.

Yellow lamplight was bobbing toward them from a driveway. A stranger was shouting. The twins got up, looked for their parents and saw them in the near distance. One of them—they never found out which—raised their arm and pointed it at the approaching light. A harsh shot cracked. There was a heavy thump, and the light fell, and then Iris and Floyd were chasing after their parents, who were already stumbling across the paddocks, heavy sacks hefted over their shoulders, not calling for their children, not looking back.

And again, and again, and again until, two years after the night of grain and murder, Iris and Floyd found themselves on the shore of a rocky bay under a white moon. Small waves were nudging their ankles. Each of them clutched a blunt wooden blade. A wooden tray sat on the pebbles beside them, filled with milky, squirming meat.

They were stealing oysters, though whether the oysters actually belonged to anyone was contestable. A local fisherman had made a claim over the shoreline that some had recognized and others had dismissed. But the fisherman was big and short-tempered and quick-fisted, so the twins had come at midnight, hoping to avoid the question of ownership altogether.

It was low tide. A long stretch of black shore was exposed to the night. Iris and Floyd stepped cautiously over the wet stones, bending whenever they saw the pale shapes of oyster shells. They used their wooden knives, which were just fire-hardened sticks, to pry the oysters open and scoop the meat out and onto the tray. The moon was full and its light strong, but clouds still moved across its face, often right when one of them was levering a shell open. In those moments of shadow the world would fade into thick darkness, just long enough for a finger to stray onto the razor edge of a freshly opened shell. They'd been there for half an hour and a dozen cuts had been sliced into their skin, releasing thin streams of blood that poured into the bay as they worked, clouding the saltwater, red mist in the murk.

When the tray was nearly overburdened with jiggling oyster meat they straightened up, stretched their spines and looked to the hills behind the shore—a reflexive movement that was no longer necessary, not now that they were rid of their parents. But they looked anyway, and it was only when they turned back to the water that they saw the blue lights winking in the waves.

They hadn't noticed them while they'd been working.

But now, standing straight and staring forward, they could see how the crest of each wave held a clutch of pulsing azure lights: luminous, erratic, brilliant. The colors flashed, fast and wild, then vanished as the water met the rocks. They would come back in the next wave, surging into life, disappearing again as the wave broke and fell.

A blue more vivid than a summer sky. They'd never seen anything like it. In their short lives, they'd scarcely stopped to focus on anything that didn't feed, warm or protect them. So, for a few moments, they stood still. For once not rushing, running, not fighting the rough grip of a hard world, doing nothing but breathing at the sea.

After a few minutes, Iris spoke. "They would have liked this."

Floyd snorted. "They would've been too drunk to even see it."

They watched the blue lights dance and roll and die. Clouds moved to cover the moon.

Iris turned to her brother. "Do you miss them?"

Floyd snorted again. Iris thought he was going to answer her, but he didn't. He waited a while, then he reached out to her, taking her palm in his. They stayed that way, facing the sparks in the waves, holding hands until the pain of their wounds and the slip of their blood made them flinch apart.

4

IRIS WOKE TO dead coals. A film of ice on her sleeping bag. Her breath pluming as fog.

She rose as the sun did, while Floyd was still asleep, still tucked up, his back to his sister. She peeled herself out of her sleeping bag, brushed the hoarfrost off her collar, pulled on boots, found gloves. There was no mist. Clouds of sheep were in the fields. An orange fuzz lingered on the eastern edge of the sky.

She began rolling up her bag, cracking the flimsy panes of ice, sliding them onto the grass. She did it quietly, trying not to disturb her brother. As she moved around the black fire pit the sun rose higher, angling fresh light onto the sandstone blocks of the homestead, imbuing their beige-blond with a lemon glow. The motes of dust floating off the stone lent an impression of ancientness, of deep time, yet not of solidity or strength; it felt to Iris like the sun was revealing the softness in the sediments, that she could reach out to the dawn-gold fibers of the rock and rub their gritty bindings apart.

Iris noticed a strange shape marring the conformity of the wall: a maroon stain, splashed across mortar and stone. From its dramatic shape she could tell that the liquid must have been hurled or splashed. And while the color was dull, its surface shone vibrantly in the light of the waking sun, like glossy paint, like holy rust. She came close to it, her mind still loose with sleep. Leaned into the stain and sniffed, and in the minerality of the rock she detected a tang of copper, a whiff of old nails. The morning shook under her feet, and the sun's weak warmth left her skin.

Not long later Floyd woke up and they prepared to ride out. In the thin air they packed, saw to their horses, broke the skin of ice on the trough and threw handfuls of chilled water at their faces, ate dried fruit, not talking until they led their mounts out of the fenced field to pause at the head of the trail.

Iris spoke first. "Rossdale, then."

Floyd looked to the ranges, tested the give in his neck. "No guarantee of work there. We could head back."

"No guarantee of work there, either."

He let out a long breath and watched it rise as mist. "We know what we're doing down there. Know who's shearing, who's herding, who's harvesting. Who needs hands. Up here we know shit."

Iris nodded. "True." Then she gave her brother a hard look. "But down there they know us, too."

Floyd met her gaze. After a few seconds he broke off and looked back to the mountains before exhaling again, loud and long. He shifted, stretched, fought off a wince.

Iris put brightness into her voice. "We've come this far." She pointed to where he was looking. "And there's a lot of money in those peaks."

Floyd's face scrunched. "You still want to go after that cat? After everything MacLaverty told us?"

"Money's money."

He closed his eyes, groaned. Then he kicked his horse into a walk. "You're buying the drinks when we get there."

Iris laughed. "Can't afford it." And she followed him, toward the snowy peaks that were starting to take on the sun's burn.

Floyd set a deliberate pace, guiding them around the largest ruts in the path, leading them toward the pass in the range that MacLaverty had shown them the previous evening. There was a tilt in his posture, a stiffness in his movements. Iris wondered how bad his back was today, considered asking him about it. But she knew he wouldn't tell her—instead he'd smile, and shake his head, and keep as much of his pain to himself as he could. She began ballasting her ambitions for what might be achieved in the day, readying herself for what might be required of her in the hours ahead.

Although he was stiff he rode steadily, and soon Iris stopped studying him and turned her eyes to the world around her. The fully risen sun built a morning of cold color, of ripped clouds, sharp light washing onto wet wool and frosted fields. It afforded the twins a confidence that they hadn't felt the previous day. With the sun unshielded, the mist absent, the land was robbed of menace. The river was no longer haunting but placid; the twisted trees appeared graceful and stoic in their contortions; the listless shepherds now seemed merely apathetic, rather than mysterious or threatening.

Iris sat high in the saddle, the bloodied sandstone behind her, the promise of the mountain gap before her. She felt like a broom had been pulled through her, stiff bristles raking her straight, clean, her mind filling with a sense of unhurried purpose. It left her content to take the day slowly, to breathe the unclouded valley in.

As she did—as the green-white light of the grass and the vast weight of the mountains filtered through her, and a pair of eagles wheeled in the distant sky—she noticed Floyd begin to twitch. He was stuttering his way through the fields, fighting his back, his horse. Iris shook the land out of her head and rode up beside him.

"Bad?"

He glanced up at her. Eyes red, skin clammy, breath short. Then he turned his face back to the trail.

Iris nodded at his posture. "Looks bad."

Floyd grunted. "I think you'll find that I look terrific."

He touched a boot against his horse's side, urging it forward. Iris was going to draw up alongside him again, but stopped when he called back to her.

"What's his first name?"

Iris frowned, puzzled. "Who?"

"This other hunter the grazier mentioned. Lees." Floyd tried to turn to look at her, but couldn't manage it. "You know him."

She felt herself flinch. "How would I know him?"

He twisted himself forward, gasping at the pain of it. "How indeed."

She snorted, tried to ignore him. But Floyd began whistling a ragged tune, made uneven by his awkward breathing. He kept at it, following no discernible rhythm or melody, until Iris groaned and called to him. "Jesus Christ, you annoy me."

He whistled louder.

"Patrick." She sighed. "Patrick Lees."

"One of your pretty fellas, is he? Likes a bath, no doubt.

Probably got a nice smell on him." He whistled again. Waited a moment before calling back. "Tall, MacLaverty said. That's not like you. Maybe your taste has changed."

"Just plain goddamn annoying." She thought about saying more, about how his taste in men was more or less the same as hers. But then she thought of his pain, and stayed quiet.

Floyd gripped his reins. Tried to laugh, couldn't quite get there. Swayed in his saddle. Sweat dark on his collar.

It took them until late morning to reach the forest at the foot of the peaks. When they got there, they were greeted by a burst of noise: rattling thunder that seemed to come from the soft ground. Iris looked down at the shaking dirt, then at Floyd—hunched over and showing no sign he could hear anything—and then at a flash of color in her peripheries. She turned and saw brown textures, white blurs, fast legs churning the dark soil. A herd of sprinting deer, moving with speed and easy grace. The thunderous noise continued, building as they came closer. There was a stag at their head, tall and antlered, leading them into the wall of trees, which they hit in leaping waves, as if they were plunging into an ocean, threading between the trunks in a way that made little sense for their bulk. They disappeared into the forest, gone moments after Iris saw them. With them went their sound, and silence slipped back into the land.

The twins followed the deer into the forest, although they stuck to the path. As they came under the shade of the trees Floyd's strength was renewed. He sat up straighter, was able to look around, and no longer looked in evident pain. His face wore only deep fatigue. At the sight of his exhaustion Iris felt her worries return. Felt the weight of his struggle creep onto her, as it always did.

This new world they'd entered wasn't what Iris expected: from a distance the deep green of the forest had made her think of wet moss and myrtles, thick ferns, spongy loam. But it had been a trick of the light: they were riding not through rainforest but into dense stands of pale, twisted trees, the same kind that they'd seen standing alone in MacLaverty's fields the day before, only now they grew in groves and thickets. The tallest of them held clutches of the same dusty blue gumleaves. Shorter varieties had green and maroon and brown colors swirling around their trunks. Others pushed out dry green needles from knots of wood that could, to an imaginative eye, have been fists. All of them seemed ancient, strong, impossibly dry. They would have been quiet, too, if not for the throngs of birds in their branches.

They were yellow-tailed black cockatoos, the same kind Iris had seen on their first day in the highlands, only now there were far more of them. A great flock was set on shredding the smallest parts of the trees. A feast lay in the seed cones, and the birds moved like they'd been in a famine, calling to each other in harshly tuneful song, oblivious to the travelers beneath them.

Iris watched them as she rode. She was transfixed by their tearing beaks, their scaly claws, the violence of their hunger, the damage they were wreaking on the trees, the painted plumage of their cheeks and tail feathers. She studied them so closely that she didn't see the change in the sky behind them. How it darkened and clouded over. Not until the cockatoos leaped from the branches, at least forty birds moving as one, trilling in panicked harmonies, winging out of the forest and down the valley. It was only then that Iris took in the danger above the forest.

"Shit." She glanced at Floyd, but his head was down, his eyes closed. His horse was instinctively following Iris's. She didn't bother talking to him; she just started searching for safety. They were still too far from the ranges to be near cliffs or caves, and it wasn't safe beneath the canopy—any one of the trees looked like they'd shed a killing limb in a half-strong breeze. So instead of shelter, she cast about for a clearing. Found something like it not far off the trail, a patch of soft buttongrass beside a jagged stump. Exposed and cold, a long way from ideal, but the wind was getting up, and the clouds were now near black.

She dismounted, hastily tethered her horse. Pulled out her canvas tent and began throwing it up. Usually they slept in separate tents, but putting up two by herself now was out of the question. She yelled at Floyd to help; he fell off his horse, stumbled over, began pegging material into the soft earth.

The rain started as they worked, with no drizzling precursor. Great pellets of icy water bulleted down on them, unfrozen but hard as hail. The wind smeared it across their faces and pulled their possessions out of their saddlebags. There was no chance of fire or dryness, no point in even thinking about it. When the tent was up they crawled into it, dragged their bags behind them and watched the rain crash down onto the canvas, pooling in the slack parts of fabric, beading on the inside of the material.

Every part of them was wet. Iris lay on her back, silently bartering with the sky. Daring it to rain harder. Beside her, Floyd had bitten down on a stick he'd brought in from the forest. He ground his teeth into the wood and squirmed through the hours of the storm. More sweat on him than rain.

*

Late in the afternoon the deluge came to a sudden stop. They listened to its lack of force, to how cascading fury had been replaced by gentle trickles and drops.

Floyd had gone still. The death of the rainstorm seemed to calm his spasming muscles, or at least give him enough peace to control them. For the past hour Iris had thought about hunting out the ointment and trying to relieve his pain, but she knew there wasn't enough room in the tent for her to work on his back. So when he spat out the stick and wriggled to the tent's door she was relieved, glad that he seemed to have overcome the worst of it.

He poked out his head and soon came back with a report. "It's clear. You should head on, make it to Rossdale by dark. I'll rest up here for the night." He pawed gingerly at his back. "Catch up to you tomorrow."

Though she was tired, Iris felt the temptation in the offer. He'd know she was tempted, too. How easy it would be to agree, to set off, fast and sure. To ride without weight. To spend a night alone in a strange town with no responsibilities, nothing anchoring her to anyone or anything. How easy her whole life might be like that.

But she knew what his offer really meant. Knew what Floyd would do in the cold shadows of the forest if she left him there. He'd made offers like this before—carefully designed to appear casual—always after a day of agony, when he could feel nothing but pain and misery, when he knew the burden of him was starting to break her.

Iris let it roll around in her, the temptation and the truth, the life she might have and the one they'd always shared, what it all meant to her: who she was and who she might become. Then she stretched her arms, settled her head. "Sounds like you're trying to use me as puma bait."

And later, when it was dark and he thought she was asleep, she listened as he climbed awkwardly out of his sleeping bag. She let him think he was getting away with it. Then she wearily got up and followed him outside, to the edge of the clearing. She let him hear her boots as they fell. She watched him stop, just as he'd started stumbling into the trees, and stared at his back in the darkness. She stayed there as he breathed and shook and sobbed a little, until he turned and slowly came back to the tent, one of her hands at his elbow holding him up, holding him steady.

5

DUSK WASN'T THE first bounty the twins had pursued. When they were eighteen they rode into a small hamlet they'd never visited before, a place in the lowlands where the forests were still thick, and soon they caught word of a once-loyal wolfhound that had fought a young bull and somehow killed it. When the bull's throat split open in its jaws the hound tasted the hot iron tang of pulsing blood for the first time and instantly gained a voracious hunger for more. It fled to the forest, and each night it would range back into the fields it had once protected, fight off the smaller cattle dogs and slaughter a calf.

The mind of its former owner began to come apart. Not only was her herd being devastated by the attacks: the wolfhound had transformed from her most devoted companion to her foulest enemy, a betrayal she could never have predicted and would never be able to comprehend. She thought she'd known the dog better than she'd known herself. It had been, in every way she understood the word, her friend.

The heartbroken grazier didn't know what to do. The cows that had lost their calves lowed all day long, and this bass chorus of grief followed her wherever she went about the property. Each morning she staggered outside to find blood, spilled organs, death. She couldn't track the hound herself—if she did, she knew she wouldn't be able to kill it, that it would either escape or rip open her own throat.

She published a notice in the local gazette, offering a small pot of money for the hound's death. That was where the twins saw it. They were hungry, out of work, low on hope. All their latest attempts at living honestly had come to nothing, either through lack of skill or poor judgment, or because people didn't want anything to do with a Renshaw. Since they'd escaped their parents the twins had briefly tried using different surnames. More often than not they were recognized—they both had their mother's stiff raven hair, and the sharp lines of Floyd's face were strikingly similar to their father's. Then they were judged not only by their parentage, but also by their lies. It was best, they'd discovered, to tell the truth.

But being honest didn't bring in a lot of work, and they were thinking of how easy it would be to go back to stealing. They could pull on their old skins and slip back into the life of their childhood, easy as breathing. So when they saw the grazier's notice, it didn't take much for Floyd to convince Iris that they should take on the job. That it couldn't be too difficult. It's a dog, he told her. A great big slobbering dog. How hard could it be?

They found the property and spoke to the wolf-hound's former master. Nobody else had inquired—the money was low, the work dangerous, and it was rumored that one of the last groups of first people were living in the forest, a band of vengeful warriors—so Iris and Floyd found that for once they had no competition. The grazier seemed unimpressed by their credentials, but she shrugged and pointed over their shoulders to the trees, telling them they'd find the hound there. She did not wish them luck.

Night followed them as they moved into the trees. In the half-light they watched a pademelon nurdle its way out into a mossy clearing. Floyd killed it with a thrown stick. He cut it open with his knife and reddened the dense moss with its blood and lay its body on the nearby soil. Then they crouched behind the hard trunk of a towering blue gum, a tree that must have been at least half a century old, broad enough to hide them both.

They watched the strewn blood and stiff corpse of the pademelon, waiting for the wolfhound to emerge. They didn't own a rifle, so each gripped a crude club. Later, nei-ther of them would say when they realized how bad this plan was—perhaps because the moment was so obvious. They watched the falling night darken the blood-soaked moss; they grew cold; they started to wonder whether the beast had slunk off into the hills; they began to fidget, and yawn, and then they felt on their necks the damp huff of the wolfhound's breath.

They gasped, shrieked, threw themselves away from the wet heat. A deep growl hit their ears, and as they turned and climbed to their feet they saw the wolfhound looming in the night. An open mouth filled with curved teeth. Harsh snarls filling the air. Eyes shining with glossy menace. A gray-black body, fur matted and shaggy, with a massive head and long limbs. A huge lurch of a creature, its snout higher than Iris's navel. Enormous power obvious in its bunched hackles.

Iris felt the blood flee her skin, and saw how laughable it would be for the two of them to try to beat this animal to death.

Yet Floyd seemed determined to try. He began swinging his club at the hound, yelling at the same time, standing as tall as he could make himself. Iris stepped forward and raised her own weapon, but didn't bother swinging it. There seemed little point; the hound could rip Floyd's club from his hand if it wanted to, could knock one of them down and go for their throat before the other could react. There was so much strength in it. So much leaking malice.

The wolfhound lowered its weight, gathering energy. Iris felt the icy blankness of terror. She waited for it to lunge, not knowing what she would do when it did.

Floyd kept swinging, kept shouting. There was a peal of panic in his voice—Iris could hear it, clear as prayer—but rather than giving in to his fear, he raised his volume and widened the arc of his club. Something in this combination of noise and action caused the wolfhound to hesitate. Its snarls paused. It began to twitch its nose between the two of them. On Floyd yelled, hoarse and violent, and at the apex of his wordless racket the wolfhound stood out of its crouch, shook its haunches and ran past them.

For a moment, they didn't move. Iris couldn't believe it. She looked to Floyd. His face showed the same things she felt: confusion, trepidation, relief. She gently knocked her club against his and tried to think of something to say. He pushed out a low whistle. Then they heard a gunshot.

They jumped, hesitated, began running through the forest toward the sound. When they scrambled out of the tree line they saw a lamp shining in the nearest field. They rushed to the fence, dropped their clubs, climbed over the wire and scrambled toward the light, where they found the woman who'd hired them.

She was kneeling beside a hump of fur, a rifle on the ground beside her. Both her hands were pressed onto the wolfhound, which was still and silent and somehow much smaller. The twins stood and stared until the grazier asked them in a soft choke to leave.

Iris thought of all this up in the highland forest, in their shared tent, in the hushed aftermath of the rainstorm. She wondered what they'd do differently now, faced with the same situation. Probably never take the bounty on, she thought. And yet, she realized, here they were, all these years later, trying to catch a creature far more dangerous than a dog, with a taste not for bull blood but human flesh. They still didn't have a rifle, they were in country they didn't know, and Floyd's back was in far worse shape.

They'd pursued the wolfhound shortly after he'd hurt it, when they hadn't realized how injured he was or how bad it would become. At the time, his back had been strong. So had the rest of him, as he swung the club pointlessly and fearlessly through the night.

6

A few hours before dawn the bad weather returned, not as rain but as sleet, sloshing into the side of the tent like foaming waves, like a sea cut white. The night cooled further, and the clouds hardened and the sleet froze into snow. The liquid thrash of sound was replaced by noiseless weight. The snow settled on the tent's roof, pushing the wet canvas toward the sleeping form of Floyd—quiet and still as a stone—and Iris, who lay awake, watching the dark shape of the snowdrift grow, watching it come for her.

When the dim light of dawn painted itself onto the tent's wall she got up, crawling under the sag of snow, pulling on boots, gloves, two scarfs. She fumbled for the door and unfastened herself into a world of numbing chill, of blinding light.

Whiteness smothered the forest. What had felt so vibrant and dangerous in the storm was now strangled by oppressive snow. It coated stone, blanketed mud and hung off branches in rounded clumps, caught mid-drip. The sky above was clear, and sunlight was glancing off the world with heatless shine.

Iris shielded her eyes and stumbled forward. Blinked at the gleam. Looked for the horses.

She saw the shape of them in a grove of trees, huddled together, noses touching. She trudged over, talking in a gentle coo. When she reached them she touched their faces and rubbed their ears and stroked the snow from their long dark eyelashes. Their blankets were damp and the horses were shivering violently. She hoped the rain hadn't soaked through the wool, but when she reached under the fabric she felt cold, wet fur.

Panic flushed through her. She pulled the blankets off, led the horses into the clearing beside the tent and began rubbing their flanks and backs with her gloves, still talking to them but now in a higher, louder voice. There was no music left in her words.

When her gloves grew soggy she pulled them off and kept rubbing, kept talking. A rustling sound came from the tent, quickly followed by Floyd, crashing out into the snow. He squinted into the brightness, saw Iris and the horses. He saw how they were shivering, saw the frozen streams of mucus on their noses. He swore, ducked back into the tent and came out with the blankets they'd slept under. He threw them at Iris and began lurching around the clearing, grabbing sticks, grabbing his back. Iris picked up the blankets and ran them across the horses, wiping and mopping. When they were wet through she tossed them aside and resumed rubbing with her hands. She closed her eyes. Sang an old rhyme. Tried to push the heat of her flesh into their bodies.

After a few moments a sudden sound stilled her hands—a loud sucking whoosh. She opened her eyes, turned, and flinched. Orange flames were leaping from the sticks Floyd had gathered, brightened by the frame of white forest. The sticks had to be wet—they *were* wet; Iris could see the dark dampness of their bark—yet the fire was taking, climbing. Floyd was hunched over it. Iris thought he was blowing on the sparks, or clutching at the sharpness in his back, but then she saw him waving his left hand at the fire. He must have burned himself in whatever demonic way he'd brought the fire to life, she thought. Then she looked closer and saw fatty globules flying from his fingers, and a thick, greasy shine on the sodden sticks, and the reality of it came together, and a new strain of sorrow found her, mingling in her throat and behind her eyes.

The fire spat and grew as each viscous drop landed in its heart. Floyd grabbed another stick and rubbed his shining hand all over it. He saw Iris watching him as he tossed it on the flames and flicked his eyes at the empty ointment jar lying on the snow by his feet. Then he brought his eyes up to meet his sister's. He held them there until she broke off the gaze and led the shaking horses toward the fire.

They sidled up to its heat. Floyd kept tossing on sticks, small ones and then thicker branches, and by the time the ointment had burned away the wood held flames of its own and coals were starting to form. Iris made rough frames from other sticks and lay the wet blankets over them. Soon a thick plume of pungent, horse-laced steam was rising in a ring from the perimeter of the fire. The twins pushed through it and raised their hands to the warmth.

When the numbness in her skin was replaced by a prickling sting, Iris picked up the jar. She peered inside and saw only a thin smear of ointment left on the bottom rim. Its lamb reek twisted into her nostrils until she took her face away, up to the white-clouded sky.

Floyd seemed to be waiting for her to speak. When she stayed quiet, he nodded at the horses. "They wouldn't have made it."

"You don't know that."

He opened his mouth, paused, said nothing. He shrugged and placed another branch into the heat.

Iris again looked into the empty jar. Despite what she'd said, she knew he was right. Not because she could tell, but because he understood horses better than she did. He always had, and it had always infuriated her. She loved hers more, cared for hers better, took more time getting to know each one they'd owned—but unfailingly, through innate skill or just instinct, he'd known more about what they needed. Floyd could read their moods, their temper-aments. He knew when they wanted hay and when they'd rather have oats. He could hear sickness in their chests where she heard only a loving heartbeat. He could look at a horse and know when it would go lame and how it would happen, even if he'd never seen the land they were about to travel over. There was a language to it, a feel, that was hidden from her. It often made her want to scream.

She held the jar in her slowly warming hand, knowing that it was the last one they had, and that they had little chance of finding any more up here, far from the larger towns. Realized that Floyd hadn't hesitated, even as his back must have rung with pain while he got the fire going. She let that knowledge sift through her until the horses grew irritated at the fire's heat and trod softly away.

Before they left she tried to convince Floyd to let her work on his back with her hands. She tried telling him that even without the ointment she might be able to knead some of the knots out of him. But he shook his head, not bothering to say out loud what they both knew: that with-out it, she'd just be shifting the pain around.

"Feels better, anyway," he said, rolling his shoulders at

her. "Bit of movement and I'll be right as rain." He began to kick out the fire, swinging his leg in a stiff lurch, and she turned away, feeling tired, feeling strengthless.

They ate a cold breakfast, packed their gear, saddled their warmed horses and stepped back through the trees to the trail they'd abandoned the night before. She remembered it being well marked, if muddied by the rain. Now it was hidden by snow, and the only sign of it was the corridor of trees that rose along what must have been its edges. Even then it wasn't always obvious, and the twins relied on their horses to find the true path, which they did, as dependable as the dawn, following the sense of navigation in their blood and the subtle contours in the land that not even Floyd could make out.

They found Rossdale at noon, after passing through the snow-muted forest, moving out of the cold shadows of the peaks and being delivered onto a vast plain of gray-blond grass. The town lay in what felt to Iris like the center of the plain, and was bigger than she had expected. Houses, shops, a tavern, a post office, a church, all ordered in a neat grid, all made with the same large sandstone blocks they'd seen in the walls of MacLaverty's homestead.

They entered through the main street, coming from the south, riding slowly. Only a handful of people were outdoors—a man and his child marching away from them; a woman pulling smoke from a small pipe; another moving past the saddlery, her arms heavy with leather. Iris noted the enforced civilization, the starkly empty gutters, the silence.

"It's too clean," she muttered to Floyd. "Doubt they'll like the look of us."

"Nobody likes the look of us." He raised a finger to his cheek, wiping off a streak of grit and grease. "Would help if you'd have a wash, every now and then."

Iris rolled her eyes. They rode on down the street, taking in the town, until the strange silence was broken by the singular sound of a grown man crying.

Floyd turned his horse toward the cries, steering down an alley. Iris followed, and when they came out into another street they found a man sobbing into cupped hands. He was standing by a stable, his horse beside him, saddled and bridled and flicking its ears, looking rested and impatient. But the man kept on crying, loud and hard, with wet ferocity, without control. Gray whiskers pushed through his fingers, darkened by tears. His hands tightened over his face, and the twins could only see his damp beard and fine clothes—long wool coat, crisp white collar, shining boots. As they neared him the sobs grew into screams, high and primal, stabbing at the air around them: a noise nothing like a voice.

Iris hung back, rattled and unsure. Floyd levered

himself out of his saddle, so she did too, but she didn't know what to do next; she had gone numb. A moment later a younger man appeared—a stablehand or servant, judging by the cut of his clothes. He came to the man's side and began talking to him, holding him by the back and shoulders. Floyd roused himself, stepped forward, took the reins of the man's horse and led it, alongside his and Iris's, into the stable. Iris watched him and became aware that she was still standing there, not moving.

The older man had been coaxed to sit down on the edge of the gutter. He seemed to be over the crest of his emotions—his screams and sobs had ceased, and he was now staring out into the street, his eyes red and puffed, his breathing slow and heavy. Iris was in his line of sight, but he didn't give any sign that he'd noticed her.

His servant did, though. Anguish and apology were spread over his face. "His son," he explained to Iris. "Last night." He pointed down the street to where the town gave way to the cold sea of grass. "Dusk took him last night."

Afterward, Iris would try to recall how long she stood there, watching the man's grief leak up from the gutter. She felt that she was bearing witness to something she couldn't or shouldn't move away from, and that in this moment the man deserved company, even the company of a stranger, although she couldn't have said why. But time didn't run right while she was there—it could have been anywhere between one and ten minutes—and all she could remember later was how empty the street felt, how enormously empty.

When she came back to herself Iris saw that although the man had stopped crying his whiskers were still dark with tears and his face was wet, and the air around them was as cold as snow, so she reached into a pocket and handed him a clean handkerchief. The man took it without looking up and pressed it hard against his eyes. Iris hovered for a moment, wanting to say something but not finding anything worth saying, so she walked away, into the stable, trying to shake the vision of him out of her.

The stalls were full, the floorboards swept, the smell more of fresh hay than manure—a scent of wealth in the cleanliness. The far end of the building was unwalled and gave way to a courtyard, where Iris could see the shapes of men. She walked past the rows of horses, stopping to nicker at hers, to warm a palm on its cheek, before coming out into the light of the yard.

The men she found there were dressed well. Not as finely as the man who'd lost his son, but their boots were polished, their hats stiff, their coats unpatched. They were standing in groups, shifting about, listless and wary. Iris looked for Floyd, but couldn't see him.

She recognized one of the groups of men. She'd seen them at the Little Rest, standing in a circle there as they were now, although this time they were not singing, not rousing each other, just standing, looking worried.

Iris walked over. They noticed her coming and moved a little, opening their circle. She nodded at them and plunged her hands into the pockets of her coat.

"Saw you fellas singing the other night."

One of them nodded back. "Did you just."

"Nice tunes." She looked at the sky. "Take it they didn't work."

The one who'd spoken frowned at her. "Come again?"

She shrugged. "If your songs worked, one of you would've killed this cat by now. And it doesn't sound like anyone's done that. Just met a fella outside who's lost his son to her." She said it airily, feigning nonchalance, but the thought of the grieving man made her look away.

Luckily they had looked away first, and the energy bristling off their bodies had died. They swayed on their heels, looked at their shining boots, until one of them— tall, heavy, mustachioed—cleared his throat.

"Saw it happen."

The first speaker flashed a scathing look at him. "You didn't at all."

The bigger man straightened up. Met his accuser's

gaze. "Saw enough. Right at sundown. One minute Errol is there, moving into the snow gums, watching the higher-up branches. I check my rifle, check the horizon. Hear a thump. Not even a big one—a little thwack, like a roo kicking off. So I turn to the sound, and Errol's not where he was. Clean gone. Then I see him on the ground a few feet away, lying all wrong, stiff as a fish. His eyes are there but they're empty, and he's being dragged back into the trees. Dusk—had to be Dusk, although I couldn't see much of her, she was already in the bracken, just a flash of tawny fur—has him by the back of the neck. She's yanking him along like he weighs nothing, and before I can say bo-peep he's gone." He paused, pulled in a breath. "Blood the only thing left. Everywhere, all over the snow."

Iris waited for one of his fellows to question or contradict him. When they didn't, she spoke up. "You didn't chase after it?"

He stared at her. "If you saw how quickly she did it. How she handled him. A grown man, and he wasn't small, Errol. Taken like a peach from a tree." There was no shame in his face. "Nobody's going after that—I don't care who you are."

A period of silence followed. Iris could feel a hard tingle on her neck, as if she was being watched or stalked.

Then the man who'd spoken first kicked at the ground. "Money's off, anyway."

Iris turned to him. "Go again?"

"Errol's father—the fella you met out front—is Lyle Horton. Richest grazier in the highlands, put up half the bounty himself. Called it off the second he heard about Errol. Can't say why. Maybe lost his nerve, maybe lost his mind, maybe doesn't want other sons taken. Doesn't matter, I suppose. Either way, the bounty's as dead as his boy."

They began muttering to each other about this, whether it was right, what would happen if Dusk killed again.

Iris opened her mouth to ask more questions, but realized she had none at hand.

She walked away from them, into the center of the yard. The story of Errol Horton's death was ballooning in her mind. For the first time since they came to the highlands, she found herself confronting what it meant to chase Dusk—the probability of being ripped into death, faster than blinking. It made her starkly aware of the softness of her flesh, the smallness of her body, the stumbling clumsiness of her humanity. The slowness of Floyd's twisted frame.

Every part of her began to prickle. She stamped her feet, rolled her shoulders and stretched her neck, which was when she finally saw her brother. He was standing in the far corner of the yard, in the shadow of the stable, talking with Patrick Lees.

*

When he saw her, his eyes fixed on her like a problem or threat. But as she came closer and more sun caught her features his face was split by a fast smile, and Patrick Lees turned toward her, tall and languid, showing his teeth.

Floyd slouched beside him, short in his shadow. When he looked at Iris he raised his eyebrows, his head angled toward Lees, but Iris gave him nothing in response.

Lees took his eyes from one to the other, until the swift light of recognition hit him.

"Ah." He looked to Floyd. "You're the brother."

Floyd's face remained still, but Iris could read the humor in him, and the dark satisfaction he was feeling at having found Lees before his sister. "So it would seem."

Lees turned back to Iris, his smile still there, his eyes finding hers. "You made it through the storm."

She tried to ignore Floyd and let herself look at Lees. Felt an elastic pull in his gaze. Resisted it, planted her feet, crossed her arms. "Didn't tell me you were going after the bounty."

"Who says I am?"

Answers came to Iris, a slew of competing lines, angry and playful and direct, but she held on to them and met his lightness and charm with a hard face, a harder look.

He waited for a moment, until he realized her silence wasn't going to give way.

"It's off, anyway. I'm sure you've heard." He nodded

at her brother. "Floyd here was asking if there's any other work around."

Iris looked at Floyd, but he was now squinting up at the sky, exaggerating the action in a way that would have been invisible to others but infuriated Iris. Lees' eyes were still on her, and she could feel the tunneling heat of them, so she took a deep breath, tried to focus on the stark facts of their situation, before looking back at him.

"And?"

Lees shrugged. "Work? Precious little." His faced swiveled west, in the direction of the grass running to the horizon. "The peat cutters are still hacking away at the bogs out west, but who knows if they're hiring. Fickle bunch at the best of times."

The taste of peat wine washed into Iris's mouth—wet copper, salt tang, smoky heat—and she found herself pulled back into that night in the Little Rest. The songs, the flames and antlered walls. The feeling of arriving in a new world, with no reputation and no commitments, unknown and unanchored. How free she'd felt, with miles of fresh ground before her. So different from how she felt now, only a few days later, with old responsibilities weighing her down, the choices she'd made crowding her in.

Lees pulled tobacco and a pipe from a pocket, a match from another. Packed his pipe, struck his match on the fence, pulled the flame into the tobacco. He took a long draw of smoke into his lungs before blowing it, blue and thick, through the air above the twins' heads.

"I'm going to sniff around the kill site tomorrow. See what I can learn about the beast. I was going to hire a scout, one of the first people, but I can't find one. They seem to have thinned out, or moved elsewhere. A shame." He sucked in more smoke. "Can either of you track?"

Iris looked at Floyd, who was still playing at having no interest. She gritted her teeth. "He can."

Lees raised an eyebrow. "That could be handy. Why don't you join me?" He looked to Iris. "Both of you."

Floyd took on a thoughtful look, rubbing his chin, either considering Lees' offer or pretending to. Or just attempting to appear contemplative to mask the discomfort in his back.

Iris knew he wasn't going to answer, so she did. "Not much point with no money on offer."

Lees smiled again, as if he knew something they didn't. "Perhaps not. But once the other graziers hear about what happened, they'll make their way here. Have a meeting. Maybe talk old Horton around." He gestured at the other men in the yard. "If they do, anyone with fresh tracks will have a head start."

"So you are chasing the bounty," said Iris, annoyance bending her voice.

Lees contemplated his pipe before slipping it back

between his lips and speaking around it. "Maybe I'm just endlessly curious."

Iris clenched her teeth, holding her irritation in. Floyd kept rubbing his chin, seeming to take in Lees' words without making any effort to respond. All of it was maddening to Iris—Floyd's stupid performance, the sudden appearance of Patrick Lees, the unmoored feeling she had while being near him, his casual offer, his playful duplicity—and she wanted to get away from both of them and from herself, so she tugged at the collar of her coat and touched her hat. "We'll think about it."

Lees nodded. "Of course." He indicated a lemon-gold building that rose above the stable. "I'm staying at the inn. I'll be leaving at first light." Another little smile. "I hope to see you then."

They left Patrick Lees breathing smoke at the plains and walked back through the stable to the street. Lyle Horton and the stablehand were gone.

Iris checked that nobody else was nearby before she turned to Floyd. "That make you feel clever?"

There was a thin sheen of sweat on his face, even in the day's chill. "He approached me." He rubbed at his neck. "How was I to know he's the fella you're keen on?"

Floyd sounded tired, looked worse. Iris didn't believe

him—there was no way he wouldn't have seen a tall stranger and not noticed the connection. But in truth she was angrier at herself, so instead of fighting with him she turned away and headed down the street.

They spent the afternoon resupplying. Food, oil and dried goods weren't hard to come by, but they were more expensive than Iris had expected. It left them with less money than she'd hoped for, which wasn't much to begin with. She began ruing the extravagance of their night at the Little Rest.

After that they went to the apothecary, looking for a jar of Floyd's ointment, not holding much hope. The man behind the counter squinted at Iris's request.

"Never heard of it, love." He frowned. "What'd you call it again?"

"Collins' Balm."

The apothecary snorted. "Sounds like snake oil."

Iris considered explaining that it was the only product that relieved the ache in her brother's back, that nothing else worked, nothing of nature and nothing of industry, but she'd told this story before and it had never helped, and the apothecary didn't seem like the sort of man who listened to women anyway. So she thanked him and returned to the street, where she shook her head at Floyd who—as she knew he would—shrugged and smiled and sauntered off as if it didn't matter, even though his saunter was pulled crooked by his pain.

Evening came fast; coldness bit deep. They considered renting a room at the inn, but quickly decided they couldn't afford it. Iris was happy to avoid being in a building full of song and drink, close to Patrick Lees, while Floyd squirmed on his back nearby. They could have camped outside town, but the tent they'd used was still wet, and neither of them was keen to share their remaining one. So they decided on an option they'd taken many times in the past: sleeping in the stalls with their horses.

They moved back through Rossdale's quiet streets. Iris wondered what the stable master would charge, if she could pay for their stay by mucking out stalls in the morning. As she mentally prepared her pitch for their services they rounded the corner to the stable and nearly strode into the unmoving figure of Lyle Horton.

He was standing in the center of the street, looking dazed. When the twins stepped around him he looked up. Dim recognition crawled over his haggard features, and as Iris passed he reached out to touch her arm.

"Ma'am," he said. "Thank you for your care earlier. I was not myself."

He was staring into her face, and he looked so drained, so spent and hollow, that Iris couldn't meet his gaze and instead looked down at the cobblestones.

"It was nothing."

He shook his head. "It was kind. Kindness is rare." He extended his hand. "Lyle Horton."

She wanted to keep walking but saw no other choice than to take his palm. "Iris Renshaw." She indicated Floyd. "This is Floyd."

His eyes slowly brightened. "Any relation?"

"He's my brother."

Being near to this man after witnessing him howl and bellow so ferociously earlier in the day made Iris uncomfortable. She wanted to keep moving, to put him and all his ragged grief behind her.

But Horton was straightening up, looking between them. "That is plain. I meant the other Renshaws—the outlaws. The killer-thieves." He peered closer at their faces. "They were around before your time, but you must have heard of them. Stole from me once, decades ago. Utter savages, the pair of them, although . . ."

His words left him as a stillness swept over the twins. He saw Floyd turn his face, saw Iris clutch on to a breath.

"Oh." Horton raised a hand to his forehead. "Of course." He shuffled back from Iris, and the gratitude in his face shifted to something far colder. "I'd forgotten they'd bred."

Floyd looked back to him and brought his hands together, as if in prayer. "Please." His voice was a soft scrape. "We know who we are."

Lyle Horton was not listening. His eyes had widened. "Their children." A wet shake came into his voice. "Growing old."

There was a great bitterness in his words, spoken not so much to the twins as to the world around them. He turned and walked away, leaving them on the brushed stones of the street, standing a few yards apart, neither of them moving.

7

IRIS KNEW HER parents had done horrific things, unforgivable things. She'd heard countless stories of their banditry, and witnessed—contributed to—many other instances. She harbored no doubts about their crimes. They were thieves. They were killers. They were what people said.

But that wasn't how Iris chose to remember them, because the truth of what they had done wasn't the truth of all that they were. She knew that Lyle Horton was right in saying that they were savage, but remembering it only brought to Iris's mind the sadness that had walked hand in hand with their savagery, all the small miseries of life outside the law. The things nobody was interested in, that had nevertheless shaped who her parents were and, in many ways, who she was. Who Floyd was.

After she and her brother freed themselves the world kept recognizing them, kept reminding them of how monstrous their parents were. But she nursed within herself a version of them they'd told her about, from a time when they were malnourished youths, living on the other side of the world in the old country, finding ways to be near each other. Lingering by the post box at dusk. Sharing milk from a porch-snatched bottle. Swinging their hands in church so that they might graze one another's knuckles. Sneaking into the nearby woods to lie on a green bank, dipping their hands into a clear stream, pulling out trout and holding them, fat and wriggling, up to each other's eyes: an act both small and catastrophic.

The woodland waters and everything in them belonged to the local viscount; to take a fish was to pilfer a coin from his purse. To be caught by his gamekeeper, as her parents were on their way home one sunny afternoon, was to be arrested; to be charged and sentenced without ever appearing in front of a judge or jury; to be locked in the crowded, foetid hold of a creaking ship and dragged in chains to the far corner of the world.

That's who Iris thought of when they came to mind: her parents as children, lying free beside running water. Her father showing her mother how to push a hand through the cold current and bend a wrist under a ledge. How to spot the mottled color of a fish against the ancient pebbles. How to mesmerize it by stroking its belly, how to gently grasp it by the body, how to pull it alive and twitching up into the forest's light. Iris liked to imagine the look that would have passed between them as her mother clutched the trout. A look of shock, of wonder, of uncontainable delight. Heat and joy passing between them as she held this living treasure, plucked from a stream that only ever belonged to itself.

Iris woke with straw in her mouth. She felt groggy, disoriented, and it wasn't until she heard the snort of her horse's breath that she swam back into herself and remembered they'd slept in the stable.

She spat out the straw, got up, brushed herself down; scratched her horse's ear, rubbed its flank, told it that it was good and clever. Then she left the stall and broke the skin of ice on the trough with her elbow, before plunging her face into the numbing water. It was a shock closer to pain than to refreshment, but she surged out of the trough vibrantly awake.

With chips of ice sharp on her chin she leaned over the next stall and saw Floyd sleeping flat and straight, his chest rising and falling in a steady rhythm. She waited for pain or discomfort to mar his features but his face stayed still, so after a few minutes she pulled a pencil and scrap of worn paper from her saddlebag and wrote him a note, telling him to rest in Rossdale. He needed it, she wrote, perhaps even deserved it. She told him where she was going and what she planned on doing there. He should wait for her; she'd be back in a day or two. She reminded him to muck out the stalls.

When she was finished she knelt by his chest and attached the note to his collar with a pin she pulled from the rough fibers of her hair. In her pocket she found most of the money she had left, which she put in his bag. She made to pull his blanket higher over his body, then worried that it would wake him, so she turned away from her brother and left.

She led her horse out onto the street, wading into thick morning fog. As she came to the front of the inn she saw another horse, another figure. Both of them clouded by wet air. When she came closer, Patrick Lees touched his hat.

"Miss Iris." A touch of something in his voice, mockery or playfulness.

"Miss?" She meant to sound stern but heard the lightness in her voice, the flirt.

Lees bowed in apology, exaggerating the movement. When he straightened up he looked around. "Where's your brother?"

"Staying put for a few days."

Lees nodded as if this made sense, as if no more questions were required. "We best start moving. Fog will clear. Should be able to reach the kill site by noon."

Iris felt suddenly small. Felt foolish, lonely. But before she could hesitate she forced some iron into her voice. "Appreciate the offer, but I'm headed elsewhere."

Lees raised his eyebrows. She stayed quiet, and after a moment he let out a sigh. "Sure know how to get a fella's hopes up."

"Seems you did that by yourself." Again she meant to sound stern; again the flirt leaked out.

Patrick Lees smiled, wistful and handsome. He climbed into his saddle, turned north and raised a hand. "Might see you back here, then. Or out there."

Iris mounted her own horse. She was tempted to watch him fade into the fog, but instead she looked west. "Might indeed."

Iris rode into the mist, across the sea of grass, no wind in her face or at her back, ice in her breath, alone but for her horse and her thoughts, which she tried to keep as clear and clean as running water. She tried not to think of Dusk, though her path was swathed in fog that could easily hide a thousand pumas. She tried not to worry about the way Errol Horton had been taken. She tried not to wonder if the bounty would be reinstated and, if it was, how mad they'd be to keep chasing it. She tried not to think of hot jaws closing around the base of her skull, snapping her spine like a dry twig, or huge claws tearing her belly skin to wet ribbons.

She tried not to think of her brother, of how at peace he'd looked in the stall that morning. Or of how he'd behaved two nights earlier, in the storm, touched all over by agony. She told herself that she'd made the right decision, that they needed some time apart, and he needed the rest. That he always did better in towns, with noise and action to distract him from himself. That he'd be safe.

She also tried not to think of Patrick Lees and what she was missing by choosing not to go with him. But what he'd said about the fog lifting returned to her, mid-morning, when he was proved right and her path across the grass became clearer.

This part of the plains had rough, rocky horizons, the kind that had become familiar to her. The grass had changed, too. Near Rossdale it was the short-stalked variety planted for sheep, but here it was a softer native grass, lush and green, almost like a cushion, spongier and more verdant than the tussocks she'd seen in the wilder parts of the plains. And the flatness of the land relented. Iris let her horse's steps fall down a dip in the terrain, expecting to find a stream and instead finding a river, dark and wide, its water flowing slowly away from the mountains in the gray distance. The river's pace calmed her, just as a similar one had a few days earlier on their way to MacLaverty's property, and she found herself wondering if it was the same one.

More arresting than any of this were the shapes rising from the ground, shapes that became clearer and more numerous as the mist dissipated. At first Iris thought they were abandoned fence posts, the remnants of failed farms. Then she noticed the difference in their sizes and shapes—some tall, some short; some straight, some curved—and thought that they were dead trees, killed long ago and whitened by time.

It took her longer than she was proud of to realize that she'd seen trees like these before, only they weren't trees: she was looking at bleached bones. They were smaller than the ones around the Little Rest, but they had the same smooth contours, the same soft glow. As she followed the river she began to see more of them, rising from the earth—cold, random, alabaster. Ribs and limbs and hips, impossibly old, haunting the green life of the country, beckoning her west.

As Iris rode through this skeletal field, cloaked by the lifting mist, she felt no settling gloom, no chilling loneliness. She felt only a stronger pulse of what she'd been feeling ever since she and Floyd had come up the passage and stepped onto the plains: the thrum of recognizing a place she'd never seen before. She felt that she fitted into this landscape, among these millennia-dead beasts, just as she'd fitted into the world around the mirror-faced tarns and cold forests and vast peaks.

The more she saw of these highlands, the more she wanted to remain among them. And as she followed the river, through the gauntlet of bones, she caught herself hoping that Floyd would want to remain up here, too. That he'd find a way through his pain. That he'd forget how one old man had recognized them. That he'd open his throat to the sky, and this place would swim into him, and he'd feel everything she felt.

At noon she stopped to let her horse drink from the river. The range had grown on the horizon, revealing craggy textures, sharp peaks, fields of snow. Between Iris and the mountains the land began to rise, morphing from grassland into something darker—not a forest or lake but a damper world of vegetation, brown and soggy, which she finally recognized as her destination.

Reaching it proved harder than she'd imagined. The soil leading up to the dark plateau was wet and treacherous, and her horse was reluctant to step into it. She tried dismounting and leading the way, but after a few strides her boots sank deep into the loam. She couldn't squelch her way forward while also convincing the horse to follow, so she returned to the riverbank and kept riding, skirting around the higher land.

For the rest of the day she followed the river, searching for a path upward, finding only sodden ground until dusk, when she came within sight of a place where the flats around the water widened. Beyond them a gradual incline rose up to the dark plateau. Iris was a fair distance away, but she could see a row of people walking down a trail in the slope, hefting long tools over their shoulders, and in the fading light they seemed to her like ghosts or reapers.

Rather than approaching them in the darkness, she made camp. She set up her tent and tethered her horse to a fossil that arced between two mounds of the cushion-like grass. She brushed the sweat from its coat, gathered armfuls of driftwood from the riverbank and lit a fire that soon leaped and crackled, warmed her hands and cooked her damper. After eating she spoke to her horse for a while. When she ran out of things to say she watched the great quilt of stars unfurl above her until they were brighter than the late-winter sun. Then she climbed into her tent and slept.

The next day she rose early, got her fire going, boiled tea, packed down, set out. The mist was thinner than the previous day's, and she could see more clearly the long wet stretch of land that ran above and away from her. But instead of heading up the slope, she continued in the same direction, beside the river, until she came around a bend and found a forest of small, conifer-like trees that looked, at a squint, like they were topped with celery. Beneath them sat a clutch of wooden houses.

Smoke rose from the neat chimneys and people were moving about in the morning light. She kept riding toward them, sitting up in her saddle, making herself obvious. When she reached the spot where the small main street ran down to the water she dismounted, tethered her horse and waited. She knew nobody who lived there, and there was no reason any of the villagers would be expecting her, but she waited anyway, looking for the right person to talk to.

Soon a group began moving in her direction, men and women and teenagers, although they showed no interest in her presence. They were holding long poles topped with short square blades, and some of them wheeled barrows and pushed larger carts. They moved past Iris, toward the slope that led to the plateau.

Iris nearly called out to them, but the quietness of these people convinced her that patience was required, and not long later she was proved right. A woman at the end of the group peeled off, approached her, hefted her ominous tool and looked Iris up and down.

"Can we aid you?"

Iris did her best to appear friendly. "Heard there might be some work on. Helping cut peat."

The stranger cocked her head. "Look like we need help?"

"I'm fit. Hardy. Can work all day and never learned how to complain."

"They should make you queen."

Iris felt disappointment move through her, disappointment and despair. "I won't waste your time, then." She nodded at the woman and turned, making to leave.

But the woman moved to stand beside Iris's horse. She held a hand to its nose, let it nuzzle her palm. "You come far?"

Iris sighed. "Feels like it."

"Doesn't it always."

The woman studied the horse's eye, as if what she found there said something vital about the character of its owner. After a moment she turned back to her companions. "Come on, then. One day."

In theory, the work was simple: lift the spade, plunge it into the peat, cut by pushing and twisting, lever a rectangular sod out of the wet earth and up into a waiting barrow. But Iris soon found that there was a technique to it that was easy to observe, yet hard to master. It had to do with the wrists, but also the legs and back. Getting it wrong meant the peat came out ragged, which meant the hole it left behind was uneven, which compromised the shape of the next sod. Ideally they were collecting uniform bricks, but most of what she cut throughout the morning came out as shaggy logs trailing stringy fibers.

Her new colleagues didn't notice, or if they did they didn't comment. They worked methodically beside her and didn't speak to her much, other than to show her what to do and where to do it. Lydia—the woman who'd hired her—seemed to be in charge, although this was only evident in the way the others deferred to her and stopped moving whenever she looked out over the bog or up at the sky. Otherwise they worked patiently in unison, neither giving nor receiving orders.

At midday they stopped to eat. Iris offered around some of the damper she had left over from the previous evening, but it was politely declined. When the rest of the cutting party brought out their own lunch, she saw why. Each of them had large bark parcels, which they opened to reveal lengths of charred meat that were still steaming. Iris felt embarrassed by her meager offering and didn't want to take any of it, wanted to pretend she was happy with her cold damper, but Lydia pushed a hunk of meat toward her in a way that made refusal seem unwise.

Iris thanked her and took the black-red flesh. It warmed and greased her fingers, and when she raised it to her mouth it came apart at her lips before it even touched her teeth. Such tenderness came from ways she couldn't fathom, because the meat was clearly wallaby—she and Floyd had eaten plenty of wallaby over the years, and while she enjoyed the gaminess it had always been tough, almost rubbery, requiring long, jaw-aching sessions of chewing before it could be swallowed. But it wasn't just the tenderness that startled her: a rich, savory depth of flavor spread through her mouth as the meat seemed to melt apart in her cheeks.

Iris gazed at her companions, wanting to know how they'd turned rough game into this soft delight, but they weren't looking at her. She wondered how long these people, and the few others left like them, had been cooking food like this. She wondered how long they'd keep doing it, how long they'd be allowed to.

After lunch the bladed shovel was gently taken from Iris and she was assigned to push one of the barrows that was used to collect the peat before it was transferred to one of the larger carts. She didn't mind; if anything, she was relieved to no longer be fumbling and failing at something. And now she could wheel her load while looking up and around at the world, the blue-green forests and sheer peaks and endless sky. The other cutters continued to pay her little attention, which she'd decided to interpret as acceptance of her companionship, rather than annoyance at her company.

After an hour one of them abruptly stopped work, knelt in the wet peat and pushed his hands into the hole he'd cut. When they saw this the others stopped, too, although a couple of them moved to help whatever he was doing. They were patient, almost uninterested. Iris tried to copy them but her curiosity soon got the better of her, and she wandered over to see what was happening.

The young cutter who'd first paused his work was carefully pulling chunks of peat out of the hole, handing them to his companions. Iris watched, unsure of what was happening until her eyes caught a pale glint in the dark soggy matter. She now saw that the cutter was removing peat from around whatever was giving off this glint. As he did, he revealed a long, broad shape, smooth and curved and white: a bone.

When he'd released most of it he levered it out of the bog and lifted it onto the surface. Iris could now see sharp, triangular protrusions on the arc of the bone. It looked like a jaw, or perhaps part of a jaw, because the protrusions could only have been teeth. The bone was as long as the young cutter's arm; the creature it had belonged to must have been impossibly large.

The others helped him out of the hole, then placed the bone in one of the larger carts. Iris laid a hand on the length of it, feeling the gritty porousness of the material.

Then she took her hand away, suddenly worried the oils in her skin would somehow stain or foul it.

She turned to the young cutter. "Do you find these often?"

He had already picked up his shovel. "Sometimes."

"What do you do with them?"

"Usually we leave them where they are. This one is in the way, so we'll take it back to the village."

"What is it?"

He stretched his arms and turned back to his work. "What it looks like."

Later in the afternoon Iris found that Lydia was pushing a cart alongside her. It might have been coincidence, but Iris felt like it was a small sign of acceptance or friendliness. After a while Iris looked at the growing stack of peat bricks in her cart, and raised her voice so Lydia could hear her.

"You turn all this into wine?"

She shook her head. "We sell it to some fellas in Rossdale. Someone else buys it off them. Guess they smoke it into grog. We keep some for building and burning, but we sell most of it on."

It wasn't the answer Iris had expected. "How long have you been doing this, then?"

"Five or six years." Lydia took in the confusion on Iris's face. "You seem surprised."

"I assumed this was something you've been doing forever. That the peat wine was your invention, an old tribal remedy or something."

Lydia shook her head, smiling grimly. "Nothing to do with us. We've used the peat forever, but selling it to you lot is a new thing." She looked out over the bog, at the small yet growing section that they had cut. "Gotta survive somehow."

Iris followed Lydia's gaze. "What's stopping others coming out here and cutting it themselves?"

Lydia shrugged. "Long way from anywhere. Unfriendly locals. Big old cat that might eat ya."

Iris let the air hold these words, and waited a while before speaking again. When she did, she tried to sound casual. "You worried about that?"

Again Lydia smiled joylessly. "Not particularly. Seems she mostly kills those who are trying to kill her. And when she's not eating men, she's eating their sheep. No sheep around the bogs. No deer, either—she and the other pumas have scared them off. Good thing, too, because they'd rip the peat up with their hooves, wreck it all in no time. Something that's been here as long as we have." Again she looked out at the far reaches of the dark plateau. "No, I quite like her. Although don't tell anyone I said that. I don't need the trouble."

*

When the afternoon light began to fail they turned back, helping each other push and pull the laden barrows and carts. Back at the village they stored the peat in a large dry shed and laid their tools by the doors of their small houses. Iris realized she was hovering in the narrow street, unsure of what to do, what was now required of her, whether her role was over or there were more tasks ahead of her. Then she felt Lydia's hand on her elbow, guiding her inside one of the houses.

"Time for a meal, I reckon."

The house was cold and sparsely furnished. Faded timber floors, timber walls, timber benches in the kitchen, a small corridor that must lead to bedrooms and an outhouse. It looked lived-in, but nobody was there.

Iris watched Lydia move to the fireplace, watched her rip a spark from her flint into a nest of leaf matter and twigs. "Just you here?"

Lydia breathed onto the sparks. Smoke plumed, flame rushed. "Just me."

Iris sat on one of the chairs by the small table. She offered to help Lydia as she moved about the room, building the fire and preparing a meal, but was rejected. When she offered again, Lydia ignored her.

A few minutes later two plates were laid on the table. Dark bread, butter, bitter leaves, more tender wallaby, although it was a different cut from the one they'd eaten for lunch—leaner, gamier, bloodier. A pot had been hung over the fire.

They ate without speaking. When the pot began to boil Lydia hooked it off the flames and poured tea. She pushed a cup to Iris and laid beside it a handful of coins.

"A day's labor. A day's wages."

Iris looked at the coins, shining dully in the firelight. She nodded in thanks and pocketed them. For a while they were silent. Iris played with the coins in her pocket.

"No more days, then."

"Afraid not."

"Can I ask why?"

Lydia blew at the steam rising from her tea. "You seem all right. Haven't done anything crook. You'd probably get better at cutting. But this is a family business"—she paused, letting the emptiness of her home fill the room— "and it barely brings in enough for us as it is. Can't be hiring anyone else. Wouldn't make sense."

"Right." Iris felt hope leaking from her body, hope she hadn't realized she'd been clutching so tightly. "Then why'd you bother taking me along today?"

Lydia took a long drink. "Said you'd come a long way."

Iris felt herself becoming upset, impatient. Her fingers were rubbing the coins against each other. "Know of any other work around? For me and another? I have family, too."

Lydia stared at her, hard but not unfriendly. She got up

with her mug and put a small log on the fire. She turned her back to it so she could warm her legs.

"You like it up here, don't you?"

Iris tilted her head back. Exhaled slowly. "I do."

A new light came into Lydia's eyes, an emotion Iris couldn't recognize—not pity and not sadness, but something similar. Recognition, maybe. Or an acknowledgment of something shared.

"Nothing I know of, but I'll ask around. See what I can find out. Can't promise anything, though—the graziers aren't in the habit of telling us much. Don't want much to do with us. Would rather we disappear."

Iris brought her hands together around her mug. Suddenly she felt selfish, petulant. "Thank you." She looked up. "And thank you for today. I'll camp by the river and head off in the morning." She drained her mug and stood to leave, but Lydia raised a hand.

"You'll sleep here tonight. Plenty of spare beds. I've already had one of the lads bring your horse round the back."

A wave of emotion hit Iris—gratitude, relief, exhaustion—and for a moment she stopped breathing.

Before they went to bed they sat up to watch the fire dwindle. The last log was wrapped with orange flames.

Then it glowed a darker color, before it began to fall apart, its hardness eaten away. Lydia stared into the coals.

"You weren't thinking of going after that cat, were you?"

Iris rubbed her eyes. "We—my brother and I—were considering it, until the bounty was called off. You heard about that?"

Lydia nodded, her expression unchanged.

While looking at her, Iris realized something. Or thought she did. "You could track her, couldn't you?"

Lydia pulled the same sad smile she'd been showing Iris all day. When she spoke, she directed her voice forward, to the dying fire.

"My father and his brothers could've. My grandfather could've done it with his eyes closed." Her smiled died. "Yes. I could track her. Even with all that you lot have taken from us, I could do it."

Iris flinched. At first she didn't know why, but then the sensation swam into clarity: *you lot.* She didn't know how to feel or what to say, so she kept to the same topic. "Then why not go after her?"

Lydia shook her head. "Like you said. Bounty's off."

"What if it's reinstated?"

"Not my business."

"Have you heard what the graziers are paying for her head?"

"Please don't talk about the graziers here."

The coals glowed a shade somewhere between ruby and

persimmon. Iris felt the air in the room shift. She became uncomfortable, too hot, too close to her host. Fidgeted in her seat. Touched her face.

"Someone will get her eventually. They'll have to, bounty or no bounty. Seems everyone but you wants her killed."

Lydia stood and picked up an iron poker. "I'm not so sure about that." She rammed it into the coals, stirring up a miniature storm of sparks. "Fella came by here recently. Had an accent. Said he'd been hired to catch Dusk, but when he asked about her it was like . . . I don't know. More like he wanted to find her. As if she was a friend he was worried about. He set off after her, but I never got the impression he wanted her dead."

Iris felt her mind turn over. "Are you talking about the Patagonian?"

Lydia kept twisting her poker into the fire, separating the last of the burning wood. "Didn't say where he was from. All I know is that he was different. Not like the rest of you."

Again Iris flinched. She spoke before she could stop herself. "A shame he's dead, then."

Lydia glanced up, a new sharpness in her expression. "He is?"

"That's what they're saying. Hasn't been heard from in weeks. But he can't still be alive. Nobody could survive that long up here."

Lydia looked at Iris, her face stony, and let Iris's words hang between them for a long time. When she spoke her tone was bitter, amused.

"That's odd." She returned the poker to its stand, angling its glowing tip away from the floorboards. "When I spoke to him it was only six days ago. Then he went on his way, heading into the mountains proper. Up where the rivers begin."

8

As Iris lay in one of Lydia's spare bunks she found that she could not sleep, even though she was tired, she was comfortable, she was safe. The day's events kept repeating in her mind: the work on the bog, the damp emergence of the jawbone, the tenderness of the meat, everything Lydia had said to her. It all muddled around in her thoughts, and then the weight of it pulled forth a memory—something that had happened when she and Floyd couldn't have been older than twelve.

They had made camp with their parents in an abandoned sandstone quarry on the coast, not far from where they'd stolen the seal oil a few years earlier. The quarry was just a cliff that had been hacked back from the water until the best of the soft, golden slabs of rock had been carved clean and carted away. The remaining sediments of the ravaged cliff were known to be loose, unstable. It was a perilous place to linger, which was why their parents had chosen to camp there. This was one of their many curious wisdoms: that finding safety often meant seeking out danger.

Floyd and their father had been hunting in the forest while Iris and their mother were collecting kelp and shellfish on the shoreline. By the time they had a full bucket of black mussels and flat strands of grass-green kelp, it was getting dark. They carried their bounty back to the crumbling cliff, built their fire, set their pot to boil.

The night deepened. Firelight flicked shadows onto the weak stone wall at their backs. The pot took on a slow simmer, and Iris laid the kelp into its steam while their mother dumped in handfuls of mussels.

At this point their parents would usually have been well into the rum. Their father on his back, eyes on the stars, mouth clenched and sticky, seemingly peaceful but ready to swing a fist or stick at anyone who disturbed him; their mother lurching around the campsite, singing a melancholy old tune, only breaking off randomly to howl at her children.

But they'd run out of rum the night before, and had no luck in replenishing their stores. No doubt this was why their father had insisted on dragging Floyd into the bush, ranting about how the boy needed to learn how to track—a distraction from his thirst more than a lesson for his son. Iris had watched them go, their strides identical, their bodies hard and thin, their faces so similar but for age, and for a moment she felt that Floyd was her father's twin, not hers.

Once they'd melded into the bush she had been left to face the afternoon and evening with their mother. The whole time she had been tense, her body ready to flinch, waiting for her mother's addiction to rise and bite, limbs and voice to lash out. But in the afternoon by the waterline, in the evening by the cliff, they spent the hours together quietly, gathering and working, her mother seemingly almost unaware of Iris's presence.

Iris didn't understand: normally a night without drink would send her mother wild. At best she should have been gripping her knees, muttering curses. But instead she was calm, her face almost reflective as she gazed at the sea and the many small islands it held, rising from the low waves all the way to the horizon, green with scrub and heavy with birdlife.

The heat of the fire bounced off the sandstone, ringing them with warmth. A briny aroma rose from the pot, mixing with the salt of the coastal air. The waves buckled on the shore, wattlebirds called to each other through the dusk, and Iris felt her wariness waning, her body relaxing. She wondered if Floyd and their father had caught anything, hoping that they had, that the old man hadn't worked himself into a rage.

Clipped words from across the pot broke her thoughts. Her mother was talking to her, beckoning her over. Iris tensed. She didn't want to go near her mother, but didn't dare disobey her, so she stood up and walked to her side, waiting for the barked instruction, the casual insult, the smack of the hand.

But her mother just asked Iris to sit in front of her, took a broken-toothed comb from her pocket and began gently dragging it through the stiff tangles of her daughter's hair. Iris was still, not wanting to antagonize her mother, not trusting that she wouldn't suddenly snap. And yet she kept combing. Months of knots and nests began to unravel, coming apart under her mother's soft, persistent hand. Twigs came out from her hair, too, and small leaves, fragments of bark, fine showers of dirt. As she worked the comb her mother told Iris that she needed to be careful with her hair, that they had the same kind—thick, curling, prone to fluffing in humidity. It was the same hair her own mother had, she said, and her grandmother. She told Iris that certain oils might help, if she were interested in such a thing, although she wasn't sure if they existed in this country.

Iris was silent, remained still. When her mother was finished, her hair was loose and light, where before it had been a rough, dense weight. She touched her curls, watched them tumble past her eyes. Her mother moved to the pot, scooped out a mug of seafood stew, rich and steaming, and passed it into her daughter's hands. Night set in as they sat side by side, drinking the broth, chewing the mussels and kelp, warmed by the heated cliff, watching the dark shapes of seabirds dive into the shadowed islands, watching the moon glow to life and pour its cold light onto the rippled sea.

In Lydia's bunk Iris rolled over, turning her face to the cooler side of her borrowed pillow. She could see the scene of that night so clearly, so vividly, and she wondered why it was returning to her. It wasn't a memory she often thought of—only an hour later Floyd and their father had returned, unsuccessful in their hunt, and their parents had screamed at each other and fought so badly that the twins had sneaked away to sleep by the shoreline, away from the sandstone's heat.

But as she squirmed she couldn't stop thinking of her mother's comb in her hair, gentle and firm. It had nothing to do with her life now, no relevance to the highlands, to the peat cutters, to Lydia's welcoming home. Yet there it was, pulsing through her thoughts, unwilling to leave. Iris looked for the reason, the connection. She thought for a while that there might be no connection at all, that it was merely the tumbling of her tired mind. She pulled her eyes closed.

Then, just as sleep swam up at her, she finally realized what it was, and that the answer lay in the bunk, in the warmth of the house, in the food in her belly, in the soft comfort that had found and settled within her all evening: Lydia had been kind to her. Quietly, unconditionally kind. That was the connection. It was that simple and that sad, because the last time anyone other than Floyd had shown Iris kindness without wanting something in return was that distant night, between the warm cliff and the moonlit sea, when her mother had combed her hair.

Her eyes opened in the darkness. Her breathing ran deep, slow. She told herself that realizing this didn't mean anything, didn't change anything. She wasn't going to stay, and once she left in the morning it was unlikely she'd ever see Lydia again. Off she would ride and her life would go on, or it wouldn't.

She thought about the peat, the bones, the mountains, the river she'd followed and the country she'd passed through. She thought about how the mist up here lifted late in the morning, like a formless veil. She thought about how she had finally arrived in a place she never wanted to leave, but where she had no real right to remain.

In the morning they found each other on the porch, drinking tea, watching the sun climb into the eastern sky. The early light glowed purple and ochre, reaching toward them across the plains and river and bog, which it had turned from a grassy wet expanse into something richer, lending the peat an amber power. Behind them, the snow on the mountains shone against the blue-dark sky.

They did not talk, but between them there was a gentle ease. It was there in the way they shared their tea, and kept their eyes on the awakening plains—a feeling of steadiness, even of comfort. Iris wondered if it would be there if she was staying, if Lydia only allowed it to hang between them because Iris would soon be gone.

When they finished the pot Iris made to leave. Lydia watched from the porch as Iris brought her horse around to the road, took off its blanket, carefully saddled it and fastened her saddlebags, briefly spoke to it, and touched its nose and neck. She stepped into her stirrup and mounted. She stared hard at the path before her for a moment, before looking back at the porch and raising a hand.

"Thank you."

Lydia raised a hand in response, then crossed her arms in her lap, looking either at Iris or the mountains behind her, overlapping each other again and again all the way to the horizon.

Iris waited, hesitating, not knowing why or what for. Then she nodded up at Lydia and rode away.

She traveled back the way she'd come, along the riverbank, this time riding not against the course of the current but with it, seeing how the river curved and widened as small tributaries fell into it, streams of ice-clear snowmelt from the mountains that darkened as they mixed with the water of the plains. Beyond the banks the mounds of cushion grass ran to the end of her sight, green and lush and undulating, and rising from them in all directions were more bones.

When Iris first came this way the mist had hidden many of them. Now she could see legions of fossils, in a greater array of shapes and sizes, tall and wide and smooth and jagged, some clustered together and others standing alone. As the trail took her away from the river they began to hem her in—hips and shins and massive jaws, similar to the one the young cutter had pulled from the peat. Rather than finding herself seduced by the strangeness of the bones, as she had previously, she felt confused and lonely and vulnerable, as if whatever creatures they'd once belonged to might swim through time, take back their flesh and devour her with a primeval, eons-old hunger.

Iris arrived in Rossdale in the late afternoon. Immediately she could tell that the atmosphere of the town had changed. There were more people on the streets, more horses, even some carriages. Iris slowed her horse. Carriages were rare in the lowlands; until now, she hadn't seen any in the highlands. Now at least five were arrayed in the main street, lined up on the cobblestones in front of the large inn.

She moved past them and made for the stable. Inside she saw to her horse and looked around for Floyd. His horse was there but she couldn't find him, so she asked a stableboy, but he hadn't seen Floyd since he'd mucked out the stalls that morning. Iris nodded, making sure to keep her face unchanged, as if this information was unsurprising or even unimportant to her. Then she peered over the stableboy's shoulder at the carriages.

"Bit of a commotion out there."

He followed her gaze. "I'll say."

"What's the occasion?"

"Graziers. All the biggest ones, anyway. Trying to figure out what to do after what happened to Errol Horton."

"I thought the bounty was off."

"It is." He turned back to his work. "Not everyone's happy about it."

Iris thanked him and walked back into the street, feeling unfocused. She'd expected to find Floyd waiting for her, as ever, with an annoyed but patient expression on his face. She'd been unprepared for his absence, and it took her a moment to shake herself straight, to come up with a plan.

She started by visiting everywhere in town she thought she might find him. In the apothecary the man behind the counter did not remember her, and hadn't seen Floyd.

The farrier shook his head, as did the blacksmith and the tanner and the proprietor of the tearoom. In the brothel she only found women, so she didn't bother asking. She returned to the stables and asked the grooms and travelers gathered in the yard, but none remembered seeing him. They were all talking about the graziers, the bounty and Dusk.

Iris returned to where the carriages sat, rich and idle. She stared up at the inn. It was the only place she hadn't searched. She thought about going in, but Floyd had never been much of a drinker, so she walked around Rossdale again, crossing its streets, peering down its alleys, checking its gutters and yards. When she'd done that she started trudging back toward the inn, but then decided to check the fields to the north of the town, in case Floyd had gone for a walk, as he sometimes did when sitting still made his back hurt.

She walked past the entrance to town, looked north and west and east across the grass, then stopped. A figure rose from the plain a few hundred yards away, moving toward her, coming down the trail. It must be Floyd— it was Floyd. Relief filled Iris, and she walked quickly toward him, just stopping herself from running.

But then she came closer and saw how easily he walked, how wrong his hat sat, how tall he was. She stopped. When Patrick Lees saw her, surprise swam onto his face, and then a little warmth, and then a small, half-hidden smile.

*

When he reached her side she fell into step with him. Lees looked at her, his strange little smile still holding. "I was hoping I'd see you."

"Then it's your lucky day." Iris tried to sound airy, but she could hear the frustration in her voice, the distraction.

"Where's your horse?"

"Where's yours?"

"I felt like a walk." He stretched his shoulders, his long arms. "It was maddening sitting around at the inn, waiting for the graziers to make up their minds. Thought I'd take in some of this highland air."

"No shortage of that." Iris looked down the path in the direction he'd come from. "Did you find the kill site?"

"I did. All the blood poor Errol left behind didn't make it too hard." He grimaced. "Beyond that I wasn't able to make out much. Seems that Dusk took him across a river and over a field of boulders. I'm sure someone could track a cat and a corpse across bare stone, but that someone is not me."

They'd re-entered the town and were walking down the main street toward the inn. Lees again let his eyes slide onto Iris. "Did you have any luck with the peat cutters?"

Iris stared at him. She hadn't told Lees where she was headed—she hadn't told anybody except Floyd. She was about to ask him if he'd spoken to her brother, if he'd seen him, until he shrugged and held up his hands, as if in apology.

"You're looking for work. You rode west."

Iris waited a moment, letting the suspicion seep out of her. "They're not hiring."

"Still not interested in joining the world, I suppose." A thoughtful expression came to Lees' face. "You didn't see any of their trackers lying around, did you?"

"No." Iris thought of Lydia's expression when she had mentioned the graziers. "No, I didn't."

"A shame. If they would just . . ." Lees' attention was taken by activity in the street before them.

Iris looked up and saw people spilling out of the inn's doors, talking and gesticulating, all seemingly in a hurry. A group of men split off from the crowd and began heading toward the stable—the choristers from the Little Rest.

"Looks like a decision's been made." Lees touched Iris's elbow, smiled down at her. "Back in a tick." He let his hand stroke her sleeve as he left her, walking in long strides toward the singers.

Iris watched him go. She felt on her arm where he had touched her. Then she looked back to the crowd in front of the inn and began searching through the faces for Floyd's.

She waited until the last person had moved onto the street, her fingers folded tight, before she gave up. Now the dread she'd been fighting off since she'd returned to Rossdale began to take hold of her, and she felt cold under the unclouded sun, and filled with a need to do something decisive, although no clear decision presented itself. Then she was thinking of the fossils haunting the plains to the west, and how there was no work out there, and how there was no work in town, none on the stations, nothing for her and Floyd up here other than old beauty haunted by new violence, and that they should have returned to the lowlands already, hungry and hopeless.

Iris told herself she'd admit this, when she found Floyd—no matter where he was, no matter what he'd done. *You were right*, she would say. *Let's go back.* She would tell him she was sorry for riding off on him, for not discussing her plan to visit the peat cutters. *Please*, she would say, *I'm sorry.* And if he laughed at the frankness of her feelings she would hit him in the jaw and say, *Don't you dare, I'm sorry, but don't you dare, I'm so sorry.*

She rubbed her wrists, swore at the street. She had never apologized to her brother before. It wasn't something they did. She was about to throw her hat on the ground when she saw a figure she recognized emerge from the inn.

Harriet MacLaverty looked less tired than when Iris had first met her. She was wearing the same fine coat, contoured to her small, hard body.

Iris walked straight to her, unthinking and desperate, and took off her hat. "Excuse me, ma'am."

MacLaverty glanced at her. Recognition came to her features, and with it a little friendliness. "Iris, wasn't it?"

"Yes, ma'am."

"How can I help?"

Iris put her hands behind her back, so that MacLaverty couldn't see how hard she was gripping the stained rim of her hat. "I'm sorry to disturb you. It's just that for the life of me I cannot locate my brother, and as you are the only person here I know that has met him, I was hoping you'd seen him."

MacLaverty's face turned thoughtful. "I haven't, I'm afraid." Sympathy and sincerity in her voice. "I'm sure I'd remember."

Iris worked to keep her face unchanged. "Thank you." She inclined her head and turned to move away, but MacLaverty's voice followed her.

"How'd you lose him?"

"He loses himself."

"You want to hunt a cat that's killed seven men, but you can't keep track of your own brother?" MacLaverty's voice was light, amused, though her words were unsparing.

Iris could have been angry or offended, but MacLaverty's teasing relaxed her. She felt herself unstiffen. "So you've reinstated the bounty."

"More than that." MacLaverty spoke around a grin. "We've doubled it."

Iris let out a low whistle. "How did you turn Lyle Horton around?"

"We didn't. We couldn't." The smile left MacLaverty's lips. "All morning he wouldn't budge. Said one son dead is one son too many. Kept repeating it, over and over, no matter what we tried. Can't blame him, I suppose. I've never liked him and I never liked Errol, to be frank, but the man has lost a child. It would be unfair to expect him to be reasonable." MacLaverty paused. She seemed to have distracted herself and was looking back at the inn.

Iris crossed her arms. "What happened, then?"

MacLaverty turned back to her. "In the end, we wore him out. The other graziers, and me. Kept trying to convince him, kept coming at him with our arguments and the hard truth: that the longer Dusk lives, the more people she'll kill. Not to mention the costs to us all, the effect on our livelihoods. We could see how exhausted he was. He didn't give in, but around midday he stopped fighting us and just stared out the window."

MacLaverty's voice had lowered. She sounded almost apologetic. "After lunch, we came back together, but he only stayed for a moment. Told us we could do what we like. That he didn't care anymore. That we could spend his money, as long as we left him out of it and left him alone." MacLaverty stared back at the inn. "Strange to see a tough old bird like him come undone. But I don't regret it. Sometimes the right decision is the hardest one."

Iris's mind filled itself with the memory of Lyle Horton's grief, his howls and screams and tears, the collapsed weight of his body perched on the gutter, the great wet bristle of his mustache, the red ache of his eyes. "If you say so."

MacLaverty nodded, more at herself than what Iris had said, and turned to face the street. "Does your brother disappear on you often?"

"Never."

MacLaverty smiled. Jaunty positivity came into her voice. "Then he can't be far."

Iris tried to smile back. For a moment they stood there, unsure. Iris was about to thank MacLaverty and leave when she heard boots hitting the cobblestones behind her. As she turned to face the sound, a hand fell on her shoulder.

"Good news. Tell you over a drink." Patrick Lees squeezed Iris's collarbone and kept walking, nodding at MacLaverty as he passed her. "Ma'am." He strode into the inn, full of purpose.

MacLaverty watched him go. "I thought you didn't know him."

Iris could feel the pressure of his hand lingering beneath her shirt. "I don't."

9

IRIS DIDN'T KNOW anyone properly, with the exception of Floyd, who she sometimes thought she knew too well. She wondered if a bit of mystery between them might have made life more interesting. Less secure, sure, but with more capacity for surprise.

Except that he had surprised her, just a few weeks before they'd come to the highlands. Iris had woken early, to the sound of a bird in distress. Before she'd left her tent she knew that the bird—probably a raven—had become caught in one of the snares they set overnight for rabbits, and was trying to free itself. And she knew that her brother would already be dealing with it, that he'd have been awake long before her.

She stumbled out onto frosted ground and saw that Floyd was walking toward the small gully where the bird screams were coming from. He was treading softly, carrying a blanket he'd taken from one of the horses. Iris pulled on her boots, began packing down her tent. From the corner of her eye she watched Floyd, assuming he would end the poor creature's pain as efficiently as possible.

With hands wrapped in the heavy blanket he stepped down the gully. The bird must have seen him, because its screams doubled in volume, rasping and furious, and a pair of massive tawny wings flashed up from the snare, far too large to belong to a raven.

Iris took a few steps, peered closer into the ditch, and saw that the snare held the thick neck of a wedge-tailed eagle, a bird the size of a hound. The rent remains of a rabbit lay on the ground before it, but the eagle was focused on trying to free itself. It was desperately tugging its head backward, but this only managed to tighten the loop biting into its dense neck plumage. Every few attempts it flared its massive wingspan, wider than a wagon.

Floyd crept toward the struggling predator, speaking in a rhythmic hush. Iris wondered how he was going to manage it. He'd have to break the eagle's neck, but she wasn't sure he'd be able to do it with his hands: the eagle was too big, too strong. If he couldn't manage it, then he'd have to suffocate the bird—a crueller method, but the only option left. And whatever he attempted, if he made one wrong move he'd expose himself to the hook of the eagle's beak or the wild slash of its talons.

She considered going to help him, but the gully was narrow; she'd probably just get in the way. So she watched on. As he came closer the eagle screamed louder, struggled harder. Iced dirt flew from its raking talons. Feathers flew in the morning air.

Floyd reached the eagle, crouched behind it and threw the blanket over its head. The bird went still. Floyd carefully stepped around its body to the snare, reached under the blanket and shifted his hands toward the eagle's neck. Iris tensed. She waited to hear the snap of a neck, or for Floyd to leap backward, blood streaming down his wrists. And this was the moment he surprised her, because neither of those things happened. He fiddled around under the blanket, his eyes closed, his lips pressed tight. The morning had gone terribly silent in the absence of the eagle's calls.

Suddenly Floyd found purchase on something. His hidden hands shifted, then yanked down in a swift motion. The eagle's wings flared again, throwing the blanket off and onto the grass, and it reared up, neck straight, freed from the snare. Floyd was knocked onto his back. With two heavy flaps the eagle lurched up into the air, awkward at first but then more graceful as it gained height. It swung up and away through the dawn as Iris stared at Floyd, who was laughing to himself in the gully, unaware that she'd seen him.

Lees was at the bar with two glasses of foamless ale in front of him. Iris was glad he hadn't bought peat wine; after staying with Lydia she would have felt strange drinking it. She sat down, picked up her glass, took a drink, waited for him to talk.

When he did, he was quiet about it. "This is it. Our chance."

The ale was warm and flat, not bitter enough to be either refreshing or unpleasant. Iris stared at it. "Those fellas running to the stable seem to think it's theirs."

"Fools and chancers." His fingers drummed the hard wood of the bar. "Once word of the new bounty spreads, proper hunters will come up after it. Experts. Killers." He turned to her. "But we've got the jump on them."

Iris let him look at her. "We, you say."

"I can't find Dusk alone. I've proven that." He lifted his fidgeting fingers and clasped them in a double fist. "You said your brother can track. You probably can, too. I'll take us to where I lost the trail, then Floyd can pick it up. We'll be days ahead of anyone else." A question came to his face. "Come to think of it, where is your brother?"

Iris took a sip. "Busy."

"Right." Lees drank too, grimacing as he swallowed. "Well, once he's not busy we'll head off, then you'll track her, and I'll shoot her."

Iris laughed into her glass. "It's that easy, is it?"

Lees leaned back. "I'm not crazy. I know the danger. But with the three of us working together, we can do it.

We won't make the same mistakes the others did. There's more than enough money to go around."

Iris didn't know if she wanted to stay or leave, if there was room in her mind to contemplate what Patrick Lees was saying to her, if he was mad or just greedy. "I'm not sure."

"We can do it," he repeated, his voice earnest, almost zealous. "You and me. And Floyd."

Iris finished her ale. She tried to think clearly, to bring some sanity into the room. "Even if we could, I still don't like it. Especially the tracking part. That's what the others did, and they weren't all alone. Errol Horton had companions, and we know how that worked out."

"You need the money."

"That we do."

"So what other options do we have?"

Iris had half-stood to leave, but as she did another glass of warm ale was placed in front of her by a barman. She hadn't seen Lees order it. As she hovered, her knees bent, staring at the brown watery liquid, thinking of Lees' strange charm, of the pull of him, of her own desperation, of life back in the lowlands, of hungry nights and sorry days, of Floyd always being there and suddenly being nowhere, of how death by puma would be horrific but quick, something came to her: a recent memory that stirred a realization, that became something like an idea.

"Only one I can think of."

She sat back down, lifted her drink and drained it in a single draw.

Lees was staring at her. "Go on."

"You remember the Patagonian?"

Lees' face smoothed over. His eyes changed and he studied Iris, as if trying to find a hidden meaning in her words. "Never met him."

"Neither have I." She received a fresh beer from the barman and swirled it for a moment, straightening her thoughts. "But he might not be as dead as everyone thinks. He passed through the peat cutters' village about a week ago. Told them he was after Dusk. He was heading up into the mountains. Said something about the source of the rivers."

"So?"

"If he's the genius the graziers thought he was, he probably knew what he was doing."

"So?"

"So maybe we don't track Dusk." Iris let her eyes hit his. "Maybe we track him."

Lees held her look, still staring at her oddly, as if she was presenting him with a test or riddle. Then he slid his gaze away, flipped a hand, and snorted. "And he's not been seen since? He's dead. He's eaten." He took another drink. "Just happened a bit more recently than we all thought."

"Maybe." Iris turned it around in her mind. "Still

seems smarter to follow his plan, whatever it was, than one that's got seven men killed."

"How does following a South American help us?"

"Might lead us to Dusk's den, rather than her hunting trails."

"Lair." Lees shifted to face the bar. "Man-eating pumas have lairs."

They sat quietly for a while, working on their ale, breathing the stale, beery air. Iris became aware of a noise coming from a different part of the building, a muffled combination of talk and clinking. There was a muted bang that might have been a fallen glass. Lees had heard it too, and was peering around the room, trying to figure out where it was coming from. As his neck bobbed and twisted, a thoughtful look crawled over his face.

He turned back to Iris. "You know, you might be right." He was smiling now, his small and mysterious smile. "I don't know why I didn't see it. Arrogance, I suppose. Always been my biggest flaw." He lifted his hand, and for a moment Iris thought he was going to place it on her knee. But instead he balled a fist and tapped it on the bar. "I knew you were tough. Didn't know you were smart, too."

Iris felt his compliment heat her, and she both did and did not enjoy it. She was going to respond, or she wasn't; she didn't know. Then another bang sounded from within the inn, this one louder, followed by swearing—a different

voice from the one they'd heard earlier. When it reached
Iris's ears her body stiffened, and she was up off her stool
without talking, without thinking. Lees tried to ask her
something as she walked toward the sound but she didn't
hear his question; if she had, she wouldn't have answered.

She stopped in the center of the room, listening closely,
looking around. When she heard the voice speak again she
followed it to a door at the back of the room. She grabbed
the handle, twisted, pushed hard and stepped into a small
private dining room. In its center was a polished table
holding a number of glasses and bottles, which surrounded
a loose stack of cards. A slow-moving puddle of peat wine
pooled beside a fallen glass. On one side of the table sat
Floyd. On another, beneath a watercolor of blue gums in a
dry summer, sat Lyle Horton.

Floyd was leaning over the table, trying to contain
the puddle with a handkerchief, failing dismally. His collar was askew and his face splotched red. Opposite him
Horton was sitting straight, gripping his glass, his silver-
black hair neat, his creamy suit starched. Glazed eyes were
the only sign that he'd been drinking. There was a severe
composure about him that had been absent when he'd
been sobbing on the street, a cultivated hardness.

When Floyd looked up and saw Iris he smiled reflex-
ively, but the joy left his face when he took her in properly.

She let enough time pass for the room to grow awkward.
Then she spoke. "I couldn't find you."

Horton turned to her. Poured a distant look onto her face. "Miss Renshaw. It's good to see you. We—"

"I looked everywhere." She was still facing Floyd.

His slack lips opened, but if Floyd had any intention of answering Iris, Horton did not let him. "Please. The fault is mine." He rapped his knuckles on the table, sending purple waves across the wood. "I had abandoned my scheduled commitments and found myself out on the street, in need of something but not knowing what that something was." The words were rolling out of him in a firm rhythm. "I still do not know, and for the rest of my days I probably won't ever find out; but out there I saw your brother, and I remembered how I had spoken to the two of you earlier in the week—after you, of all people, had shown me such kindness. And I regretted it, Miss Renshaw, I regretted it." He kept staring at her, as if forcing an apology through the wine-laced air, although he didn't actually say sorry. "I insisted that I buy him a drink. I gave him no choice. And when he could see that I was still not my best self, he agreed to help me see off the afternoon with a game of cards. So, please: do not show him anger."

Iris had no interest in listening to Horton, even less in having a conversation with him. She wanted Floyd to stand up and leave with her, and failing that she wanted to drag him out by his collar. But Floyd was staring at the puddle of wine and Horton was focusing on her, waiting for a response.

She took a deep breath and tried to settle herself, tried to think of something polite but concise to say to the man. Nothing came to her: she was too furious, too distracted. She took a second breath, and as she was about to tell Horton that she needed her brother's help with an urgent matter, the old man spoke again.

"You heard what happened to my boy." He straightened, sat higher in his seat, suddenly alive with emotion, horribly alive.

Iris's anger stilled. "Yes." She inclined her head. "A tragedy. My deepest sympathies, sir."

"Thank you." He drained his glass and reached for the bottle. "I imagine the bounty has been reissued by now. I did not bother fighting them any further. I'd like nothing more than to see the beast dead—if it appeared in front of me now I'd shoot it, I wouldn't stop shooting, I'd fill the bitch thing with lead—but sending more people into its jaws is folly. Even I can see that."

He slanted the neck of the bottle into his glass. "In any case, it doesn't matter. Floyd here told me you've decided not to go after her. A good decision, Miss Renshaw. And as for your need of employment, you'll find work elsewhere, I'm sure of it." Again his firm eyes trained on her, now running up and down her body. "Two hard workers like you. I wish I had a job to offer you—perhaps in the future, I will."

The wine glugged into Horton's glass. Iris watched it

collect in the bottom. "That's very good of you. We won't forget it."

Floyd looked relieved, like he'd got away with something, and it brought back her anger in a red wave. She stared at Horton. "But we need work now."

For the first time since they'd entered the room he looked rattled. "Surely you're joking." He drained his glass. Then he turned his face away from her, just as the stiffness of his expression began to crack. "They told me what that cat did to Errol. How she opened him up." Again he reached for the bottle. "Nobody should die like that." He refilled his glass, not bothering with Floyd's. "Not even a Renshaw."

At last Floyd levered himself out of his chair and staggered to Iris's side. She wanted to cuff him, she wanted to hit him, she wanted to leave the room as fast as they could. But Floyd had paused. He was staring at the doorway. Iris turned and saw Patrick Lees leaning against the doorframe, arms crossed, head cocked, face inscrutable.

10

THEIR PARENTS HAD always stayed together, from the moment they were coughed out of the foul darkness of the prison ship onto a white beach hemmed by soaring cliffs, half-dead, gums bloody with scurvy. But though they were sick and weak and could barely walk, on that bright sand they reached for each other, and once their damp palms made contact they did not let go.

They remained together as they were marched in chains to a jail that had been carved into the cliff, a place of wet rock and dank air, so close to the cold harbor that waves washed into their cells each high tide, carrying enormous sea stars that sucked onto their legs as they slept. Side by side they split rocks, scrubbed floors, hauled carts of coal, chopped wood, received kickings, received lashings. Together they bled and scarred and cried, and together they eventually escaped, knifing a drunk overseer, swimming across an icy bay, wading through a black marsh and sprinting across cold fields of frosted sedge. They were both fifteen.

They slept in caves and beneath fallen gums and sometimes, on warm nights, on the sun-heated sands of the white beaches. They survived by stealing from the graziers and loggers and other would-be landowners. They stole with stealth, deception, distraction, intimidation, violence—whatever worked. Whatever fed and clothed and warmed them. They thought it wouldn't last long, that they'd be caught and killed. If they managed to stay free, they thought they'd be able to slip into new identities and live quietly on the margins of this brutal fledgling society.

But their escape had gained them notoriety, and their crimes gained them infamy, and soon whatever hope they had of settling down was gone. Later, others would talk about the pair's lives with a hint of romance, but in reality they were usually hungry and ill and despondent, and they only ever learned two ways to cope with it all: by staying together, and by drinking whatever rum they could get their hands on.

Rum had been around the jail; it was the only solace available to prisoners. Like everyone else they'd used it as liberally as they could, and they hadn't noticed the grip it had on them until that hold was absolute. Out in the world they took to drinking as fiercely as they took to staying alive, and within a few years they were no longer drinking to survive but surviving to drink. Addiction turned them reckless, opportunistic, vicious. The few friends they'd made quickly abandoned them, but together they kept going, from picked pocket to break-in, crop theft to hold-up. Together they stole oil and grain and wool and flecks of river gold. Together, around this time, they made the twins.

It was the greatest lesson their parents ever taught the twins: the benefits of sticking together. So when they freed themselves of their mother and father, that's what Iris and Floyd did. They said it to each other, the first morning they were on their own, dripping wet and shivering by a fast river. They swore that they would stay beside each other, that they would face the world together and not alone, never alone. They hadn't needed to say it out loud but they did.

The memory of this exchange flared through Iris as she dragged Floyd from the inn to the stable, having bid goodnight to Patrick Lees before he could ask any questions. Floyd's arm was heavy across her shoulders and his breath was sour in her face, but it couldn't distract her from the thought of them, twenty years younger, agreeing to stay by each other's side. And as she dumped him into his stall, she felt a rush of anger at how she hadn't been able to find him earlier. How he hadn't left a note for her. How he could've been anywhere. How she'd come upon him by accident, in the company of a man who'd treated them callously, with contempt. How he'd been as drunk as their parents used to get. How he'd not thought of her, not for a second.

But as she lay in her own stall, unable to sleep, she couldn't avoid a gnaw of truth: that she had been the one who left first. Though she had written Floyd a message, she told herself. She had given him space and time to rest while she had gone in search of work for the both of them. She had been responsible and he had been selfish. Within the flashing storm of her mind she said it silently, again and again, until at last she fell asleep.

They left at dawn, heading northwest, the steam of their horses cutting through the harshly cold air as they rode across frosted paddocks that soon gave way to plains of soft, snow-dusted buttongrass. The sun slanted onto their backs but did not warm them. Iris was in the lead, Patrick Lees behind her, Floyd far to the rear.

She had thought it would be quickest for them to

follow the same path she'd taken to the peat cutters' village. From there they could ask Lydia more details about the Patagonian's intended route and follow that course until they picked up his trail. But when she had mentioned it as they were preparing to leave, Lees had shaken his head, pulled out a map and shown them that they could reach the foot of the far western range by cutting northwest across the plains. They'd save half a day going this way, he'd said, and they would arrive at a confluence of rivers that the Patagonian couldn't have missed. From there they'd find his tracks. He said this with a shrug, with an idle pull on his pipe. As if it would be easy.

Iris didn't like the sound of it. There was no guarantee that the Patagonian would have headed to this confluence, no matter how certain Lees made it sound. And she'd liked the idea of riding back to the village, of seeing Lydia again. But as she'd considered that plan she saw how Lydia would see the three of them and would know, before they even asked about the Patagonian, what their purpose was. A look would cross her face—disappointment, world-weariness, maybe even disgust. She might help them and she might not, but either way that look on her face would remain, and it would contain truths that Iris didn't want to confront, that she never wanted to confront. She didn't think she could go on if she saw it. So she'd agreed to Lees' route.

He had nodded sagely, as if she'd made an intelligent

decision, then turned to her brother. "You happy with this, Floyd?"

Floyd gave no indication of being happy about anything. He didn't even look at Lees when the man sought his opinion. He just watched Iris mount, and when she seemed ready to ride he followed suit.

Iris ignored him. She'd ignored him from the moment they woke up, except to lean over his stall and tell him they were going after the bounty with Lees. She'd said it as a directive. When he'd stared at her in response, eyes bloodshot and awash with pain and sorrow, she had spat out a few details about following the Patagonian's trail. He hadn't replied. He had just kept staring.

The chill did not leave the air until late morning. By then they had left the grasslands behind and were moving through country that reminded Iris of the plain they'd encountered when they first rode up into the highlands. Rock and water had come to dominate the landscape: broken boulders, fields of snow, mossy stones, mirror tarns and among it all little rivulets, trickling through the land as glassy arteries. Trees appeared only as solitary sentinels or in small groves, never as forests, and they were small, gnarled by time and weather, their twisting limbs clutching bunches of dry green needles.

Here and there Iris could see bones between the boulders, sometimes rising straight up from the still waters. Patrick Lees didn't seem to notice them, or if he did he made no comment. Floyd must have seen them, no matter how hard his head was throbbing, but he remained mute.

As they rode, Iris tried not to let the land affect her, tried not to let its soft colors seep into her. She reminded herself that she would be leaving it behind her soon, either through the jaws of Dusk or with more money than she'd ever dreamed of. She worked hard to see ugliness in the tumbled rocks and soggy ground, death in the fossilized bones. It was bad country, she told herself, that couldn't be grazed or plowed. She tried to see bleakness and stark misery all around her, and when she couldn't she rode with eyes closed, trusting her horse, telling it in a small voice that it was clever and that she loved it.

The way Lees had looked at her from the doorway when Lyle Horton had said their surname kept coming back to her throughout the morning, and she found herself waiting for him to say something about it. But other than discussing their route before they set out, he hadn't spoken at all. This didn't sit well with her; she wanted to get whatever conversation they might have over and done with.

She hoped he would bring it up when they stopped

for lunch. But when they tethered their horses beside a small tarn Lees looked briefly at Iris, then at Floyd, and wandered away around the water's edge, taking great care to study the distant mountains. Iris watched him go, wondering if he was playing some kind of game with her. Then she heard Floyd stumbling to her side, and realized that Lees had felt the sourness between the twins and was giving them room to address it.

She would rather have gone with Lees and tallied up every crime her parents committed than talk to Floyd at this moment, but it couldn't be avoided. She sat at the edge of the tarn. He eased his body down beside hers.

They watched the unmoving water, the clouds reflected in the tarn's surface. They chewed old damper, passing the crust back and forth. When it was finished, Floyd cleared his throat. "I thought he might give us a job. Horton."

Iris kept her eye on the mirrored clouds. "When was the last time either of us got a job by drinking a barrel of wine?"

Floyd scratched a shin. "He was pouring. I thought it wise to go along with him." He raised his hands, half explaining, half apologizing. "By the time I learned he had no work on I'd had a few too many."

"A few."

Floyd was quiet for a while. "I thought it might help," he eventually said. When Iris looked at him he gestured at his back.

"Did it?"

"It did, actually." His face was tired. "At the time."

They sat in silence for a while. Iris was about to point out a giant bone that looked like a femur skewing out of the ground, but Floyd spoke first. "No luck out on the bog, then."

"No."

"Ah, well." He leaned forward, filled his waterskin from the tarn. "It was a good idea. So's this one. We'll probably die, but it's sound. Some of your best work."

She filled her skin too. Ripples spread from its lip across the water. "How do you know it's my plan?"

"Got you all over it." Floyd looked over at Patrick Lees, who was still appraising the mountains. "Not him."

Iris followed Floyd's gaze. Lees was walking leisurely at the far side of the tarn, hands in his pockets. "He seems steady enough."

Floyd climbed to his feet. It took him a while to drag his eyes off Lees and start walking back to their horses.

Iris felt the doubt radiating from him, and then she was speaking again, even though she didn't want to. "We were out of options."

Floyd kept walking, calling back over his shoulder. "You sure about that?"

She stood, caught up to him, striding fast and straight where he couldn't. She was angry again—angry and tired and still hungry. "You should have left word at the stable."

He studied his horse, running his eyes over its mouth, its nose, its legs. He picked up each hoof and peered at each shoe. Then he fought his way up into the saddle.

"You shouldn't have ridden off on me."

They rode through the afternoon, going fast, Lees now in the lead. The western range crept closer, taking up more of the sky until they could make out individual features and formations in the peaks. The gray cragging rock was pocked by slabs of snow and ice, and between them water was running freely down gullies, sometimes as rivulets but more often as distant waterfalls whose crashing voices became louder and fiercer the closer they came to the range.

And just as Iris had nearly convinced herself that this country had no hold over her, the landscape changed again. The scattered rocks and silvery tarns were pushed apart by a tall forest, green and thick, that formed a lush border between plain and mountain. Their path took them straight into the trees, which were broad-trunked, small-leafed, and covered all over by verdant carpets and curtains of lichen. Their branches spread as much horizontally as vertically, creating a thickly intertwined canopy. Their roots snaked through the forest floor, which was made spongy and slippery by a layer of fallen leaves. Fungus of all kinds and colors sprang out of the vegetation, from the ground and from the wood—decaying logs and living limbs. Red lips and gray ears of fungus, blue and orange mushrooms, tiny white tentacles worming their way into the world. Climbing among the trees were ferns taller than Patrick Lees, shepherding their passage, drooping fronds over them that curled down to brush their cheeks and scalps with a rasping, dewy touch.

They moved through the forest for three hours, their going made slow by the winding path and the thickness of the trees. Still they didn't talk, although their silence was now more solemn and somehow reverent. Even Floyd sat straighter in his saddle, reaching out to touch the dipping fronds, to stroke the mossy trunks. Iris tried to think of where this place reminded her of, until she realized it didn't remind her of anywhere at all.

Lees had swung his rifle around from his shoulder and was riding with it across his lap, his eyes darting about the greenery, tension and fear evident in his rigid body. It almost made Iris laugh; in a forest like this there was no amount of watchfulness, no degree of caution that could prepare them for a sudden attack. If Dusk were here, they were at her mercy.

But if she was watching them, she let them be, and soon the roar of the waterfalls, which had risen and fallen in volume depending on the direction of the path, became clearer. The forest let in more light, they could see more of the clouded sky through the interlocked branches, and then they were delivered out of the trees and onto the banks of a wide river the color of tea, and the air all around them was filled with the thunder of falling water. At first they couldn't see where this noise was coming from, but Patrick Lees led them onward, around a bend, and there they saw it.

The river curled around to the south, into more forest. But before it did it was joined by a second, pure and clean in color, crystal blue in its shallows but cut into white foam on its surface by its wild pace. It was being fed by the largest waterfall Iris had ever seen, a torrent of water jetting out from a black gap in the mountain and smashing down into the pale river below. It was loud enough to drown out any other sound.

They stopped their horses and watched, mesmerized by the torrent of falling water and the power of its impact. It was so fast, so relentless, and as she stared at it Iris began to sweat and fidget and itch. She wanted to block her ears but knew how childish it would look, so she kept her arms by her side and chewed on the inside of her mouth.

After a while she became aware that Patrick Lees was speaking to her. She leaned over to him, trying to make out his words while keeping her eyes on the falls.

"This is it," he shouted, gesturing at the place where the rivers met, where their colors mingled. "The confluence."

*

When they stopped watching the waterfall, the day was coming to an end. The sun had dipped behind the mountains and the light it threw over the peaks was a weak dusty orange. At Lees' suggestion they rode away from the falls, past the confluence, down the darker of the two rivers until they reached a high bank suitable for making camp. They collected wood, struck flint, boiled tea, cooked beans and damper, then ate and drank and fed the fire. They didn't talk much—Iris could sense that Lees wanted to, but had judged it better to keep quiet. He did ask if they'd seen any tracks when they arrived, and Iris had shaken her head. Floyd hadn't answered.

After they'd eaten it was properly dark, the air bitterly cold. Patrick Lees put an armful of fallen branches onto the coals, said goodnight to the twins and began setting up his tent not far from the flames. Iris did the same on the opposite side of the fire pit. There was more than enough room on the bank for Floyd to do the same, but he stood up and led his horse away from the heat, back toward the waterfall.

Iris watched him go. Pitching a tent away from camp was something the twins did to allow the other privacy while they were traveling with company, but they'd always done it with at least a tacit understanding between the two of them. What Floyd was doing now was presumptuous. And by heading back toward the waterfall's roar he was, to Iris's mind, being crass and obvious and judgmental, rather than tactful. She watched him find a flat piece of land, tether his horse and start unpacking his tent. Saw how he didn't look back at her, even though she was standing tall in front of the firelight. She thought about going over there, to spit and snap at him. Then she saw the familiar stiffness in his movements and turned away.

She yanked at her canvas, hammered at her pegs. By the time she was finished, Lees had already disappeared inside his tent. She loaded the fire with more wood, drank the dregs of the tea. She looked at Lees' tent and then ducked into her own, crawled beneath her blankets, pushed her head into her folded-up coat and closed her eyes.

She tried to breathe slowly, tried to forget about where she was and who she was near and how he was making her feel. She imagined a herd of deer running ceaselessly across a broad plain, their legs synchronized and mesmer-izing, a deep and earthy rhythm rising from the thrum of their hooves. She imagined the fire on the other side of the canvas, its flames jumping before flickering smaller, then disappearing, and then how the coals would glow for a while before winking out and crumbling into cold ash. She imagined herself as a tree, lichen-stamped and twisted, tall and still. And when none of that worked she got up, walked out into the night and let herself into Patrick Lees' tent.

He rose from his blankets as she approached, but she pushed him back down. He tried talking but she shook her head, pulled off her shirt, then her pants, then lowered herself to him. Her palms pushed into his chest, and she could feel the firmness and broadness of him. Then she grabbed his hands, pulled hard, guided them where she wanted. He moved up at her. She exhaled, reached back and shifted down onto him, rocking slowly and then fast, shoving his shoulders if he got too eager. She didn't look down much. Mostly her eyes were closed as she moved above him. He tried a bit of kissing, a bit of biting; he tried to roll over at various points. But she stayed on top, moving him at her tempo, moving until she had what all the blood in her wanted.

Later, as they lay beside each other, breathing trapped sweat, she stopped his fingers from playing with the old knots in her hair and turned to him.

"You haven't asked about us."

He remained still, his face pointing up at the damp canvas. "What would I ask?"

"You heard what Horton said. You know who our parents were."

For a while he didn't answer. Then he reached through the darkness, fumbling at her side until he found her small, hard hand, which he took into his own large one. "You told me your name at the Little Rest." He squeezed, his skin rough, his touch gentle. "I've known who you are since the moment we met."

11

IRIS WAS WOKEN by the waterfall in the early morning. Rain must have fallen in the mountains, or a drift of snow must have slid into a high tributary and melted, because the sound had intensified. Or perhaps there had been no rain or snowmelt; perhaps the sound was the same, and it was always going to wake Iris at some point in the night.

Patrick Lees was sleeping beside her. She reached out and felt his neck, the calm pump of his breath. With her hand on his firm chest she began thinking about the day ahead of them. If Floyd found tracks, and if Lydia had told them the truth, they would surely follow the clear river up into the peaks. She thought of how hard the terrain would be to cross, how close they'd be to all that rushing water. As she imagined it she closed her eyes and tried to match her breathing to Lees.'

*

Her family had once tried to cross a rough stream in early winter. The previous day had been black with storms; the water wasn't deep but it was fast and unpredictable, cutting through the forest they were in with furious power. It would have been foolish to step into it even if they had known the stream well, and Iris and her family had never seen it before. Also, her parents had been drinking since dawn.

This was rare, even for them—usually they started working on the rum after they were done with whatever job they'd pulled. But they'd had no luck in stealing for weeks: dry fields, well-armed travelers, alert hounds, coinless victims. On a few occasions they'd been lucky to escape with their lives. They had no money or food but they did have drink, which they'd been using liberally, morning and night, even as they rode through hard country on the lookout for anyone and anything to rob.

The twins had tried telling them to find a safer crossing, but they'd been ignored. At seventeen, they were still treated like children; when they said or did anything even remotely mature their mother and father would stare at them like they were strangers, as if time had crept up and slapped them.

So when their father thrashed into the white water and Iris asked him to come back, he didn't. He'd kept going until he stumbled into a swirling pool that reached his waist. As he'd sworn and shivered their mother had reached down to help him, but when she gripped his collar the rum gripped her, and she fell in on top of him. For a while it was comical—she beating her arms at his head, he spitting water in her face as he tried to stay steady. The twins watched from the bank, waiting for their parents to settle enough so they could fish them out.

A foaming torrent splashed up into their father's eyes. He raised his hands to his face, and was pushed backward by the surging current. Their mother's hands were still clawed onto his collar, so as he tipped out of the pool and into the run of the stream, she went with him. Their combined weight increased their speed, and within moments they were tumbling through small rapids and gullies, crashing into wet rock and each other, their bodies a tangled mess, their shouts muted by the water's call.

The twins gave chase, running down the bank, crying out. Ahead Iris could see the stream widen and deepen and give way to larger rapids, flushing with waves. She stopped running. Held her breath. Glanced at Floyd, who'd come to her side, and as fear rose in her she looked to him for a plan, an answer, some kind of action, but instead she saw in his face only a grim understanding, and then her thoughts caught up to his.

They had been talking for years about getting away from their parents: at first not seriously, only as idle dreams, but recently their mother had forced them to push a knife against the throat of a limping woman, and their father had made them steal small apples from a too-thin orchardist, and they'd both forced the twins to hold down an old beekeeper as they kicked the location of his hives out of him. So the twins had started discussing real ideas of escape, of running and hiding and disguising themselves, although they hadn't got a serious plan together, not until this morning, this moment, as their parents bobbed in the cut-up current behind them; only now did Iris see that this was how it was going to happen.

Iris felt herself become cold. Floyd put a hand on her shoulder and told her to look away. She knew he was right, and that even if they should help their parents, they probably couldn't. What was happening was out of her control, she told herself. It was an accident, but perhaps not a terrible one—awful things happened in the lowland forests every day, and many of her parents' victims wouldn't consider their deaths awful.

She pulled in a breath, closed her eyes. She tried to force herself to be still, to count to one hundred. But before she reached ten she heard her mother shout, her voice gurgling the water in her throat, and Iris remembered how, only a few nights earlier, when a fever had sheened her with sweat, her mother had run a cool wet rag across her face. And she thought of how whenever they had sugar her father would sneak it into her tea, wait for Iris to look up after her first sip, thrilled by the sudden sweetness, and give her a small wink. And she remembered how, when she and Floyd were very young, their mother and father would carry them through the endless bush when they were too tired to walk, passing the twins like precious cargo, kissing them on their foreheads, tickling the soles of their dirty feet. She remembered the trees she could see over her mother's shoulder, blurring into a green-speckled smudge as she fell asleep against the warm press of the now-drowning woman's neck. With a hot lurch of her stomach, she remembered the firm but gentle tug of her mother's comb in her tangled hair.

Sharp needles were in her eyes, her skin, her throat. Iris turned, threw off Floyd's hand and leaped into the stream's teeth.

Despite the roar of the water, Iris fell back to sleep. When she woke it was light, and Patrick Lees was gone. She found her clothes, wriggled into them, tied back her hair and climbed out of his tent.

Lees and Floyd were up and about, seeing to their horses, moving around the camp. Floyd had taken down his tent and looked ready to go, while Lees was chewing his breakfast and fiddling with the strappings of his saddle. Lees smiled in her direction, but Floyd only glanced at her, then at Lees' tent, then back at the river. She strode to her tent and began to pack it down, her movements swift and tense. Lees seemed to read her mood and began working on his own tent. It didn't take either of them long, and then they had little choice but to lead their horses over to Floyd, who had moved back toward the waterfall.

When they reached him he stared hard at the tree line, then gestured at the riverbank.

"Someone was here. Can't tell you if it was the South American, but someone came this way. Bit over a week ago, would be my guess."

Lees nodded. "Has to be him."

"Maybe." Floyd shrugged. "Whoever it was, they weren't alone."

Lees kept nodding. "Must have brought a servant." He was looking around the bank, brimming with energy. "Where do the tracks lead?"

Floyd pointed to the forested slope beside the waterfall. "Up there."

"Grand." Lees grinned. Looked at Iris, then back at Floyd. Saw how they were avoiding being near each other, but didn't seem to think much of it. "Lead the way."

They walked against the course of the ice-pale river, moving onto ground that was steeper and rockier than the trail they'd followed the previous afternoon. At first they tried to ride but the horses hesitated on the rough terrain, so they dismounted and led them by their bridles, coaxing them over fallen logs and around boulders while speaking to them in gentle encouragements and low coos.

The forest was still wet and dark but the higher they climbed, the thinner it became; the trees were shorter and drier, and lost their hanging lichen and carpets of moss. Soon their limbs stopped linking together in a webbed canopy, and Iris could see straight up to the snowy peaks, no longer distant and majestic but looming above them, sudden and sheer, cutting off huge slices of sky.

Through the thinning forest ran the river, clear and fast and cold even to look at. Its bed of gray rocks sharpened the whiteness of the waves breaking on the surface. Iris tried not to look at or think about the river. She tried not to think about much at all—not the trail, not Dusk, or the previous night, or how in the morning Patrick Lees had left the tent without bothering to wake her. She focused on keeping her horse sure-footed and avoided looking at him, although she noticed that he'd slung his rifle over his shoulder, even though it was swinging into his hip and snagging on branches. She saw, too, how his eyes were flicking around the trees and peaks, and that his posture was rigid and alert.

Later it began to rain, a chilly mizzle that grew into cold spitting drops and then a steady downpour. When it became unbearable Floyd led them to shelter beneath a stand of tall myrtles, next to a part of the river that widened and slowed into a blue pool below a series of cascading rapids. They crouched in the crux of the trees' vast root system, watching the rain pelt the river. There was no choice but to sit beside each other. Iris could feel how close she was to both of them, Floyd motionless on her left and Lees nudging warm on her right, and she found herself giving her attention to the river she'd been trying to avoid all morning, wondering about the pull of its current.

As soon as the deluge weakened Iris stepped out of the myrtles' embrace, walked down to the pool and opened her waterskin. As it filled she heard the crunch of a boot, and then Floyd was crouching beside her, dipping his face to drink directly from the river. He'd come close but wasn't looking at her, and Iris couldn't tell what he was up to, what this closeness meant. She knew they were still upset with each other but she was tired, and hungry, and things had reached a point where it was unclear to her precisely why she was mad at him and he mad at her— the actions were clear, but the motivations and emotions behind them were not—and she couldn't be sure anymore if she was in the right or wrong, if one of them needed to apologize or if they could let time take care of it.

Just as she was thrashing it all out in her mind he stopped drinking and spoke, although he kept his face pointed at the water. "We're being watched."

Iris felt herself go still. Then she realized how conspicuously stiff she must look, and forced herself to relax, to keep filling her skin. "Where?"

Floyd took another slurp. "The ledge above the pool. To the right."

Iris watched the bubbles rise around her wrist. "How long?"

"Only saw them when we stopped under those trees." Floyd pulled himself up, wiped his chin. "Could've been since we got here. Could've been all day."

Iris was about to lean back and stretch her neck, which would give her a brief glimpse of the rock above the rapids. But then there was a thumping, a heaving of breath, and Patrick Lees crashed down beside them.

He began filling his skin. Floyd stared at him. Iris ignored him; she wanted to figure out who or what was watching them before she said or did anything else. But Lees had noticed the strangeness of their silence and was looking at them, his eyes narrowing, so she took another drink and muttered: "We're not alone."

He reacted exactly as she'd hoped he wouldn't: by peering around the pool in a way he evidently felt was subtle but very much wasn't.

Floyd closed his eyes.

Iris forced a laugh. "On the ledge above the water." She patted his arm and laughed again. "Don't look right away."

Lees caught on and laughed with her, tipping his head back. When he corrected his neck he stared directly at the ledge.

"It's her."

He began fondling his rifle, swinging it round to the front of his body.

Floyd splashed water up onto his face and began to shout-whisper. "Are you blind? That's no puma."

Now Lees had the gun in his hands. "It's Dusk. I'm sure of it."

Iris still hadn't seen who or what was watching them. She glanced up, ran her eyes across the rapids until she made out a dark, hunched figure. "Doesn't look like a cat to me."

Lees paused to look at her. He showed her one of his closed-lip smiles. "Trust me." He raised the rifle, pointed it at the ledge.

Floyd tensed, but he was too far away from Lees to intervene.

Iris was between the two of them. She looked again at the watching figure, and saw only a black shape, not necessarily human. She felt Lees steady beside her. Saw him squeezing the trigger. Saw the little smile on the lips, the deliberate mystery of it, and she was reminded of all his little mysteries and deceptions, how he always kept the truth at arm's length from her, and then she threw up her hand, hitting the barrel, knocking it off target just as he fired. The shot barked through the forest, and a shard of rock split off the ledge opposite and crashed down into the pool.

Lees glared at Iris, furious, his face white with a malice she'd not seen on him before. He rose from his crouch and kicked her in the chest, his boot smacking into the flesh of her right breast, sending her sprawling. Then he fumbled with his rifle, but Floyd—who had moved straight to Iris's side—began to shout.

"Look, you fool."

He was speaking to Lees, but from her position in the dirt, clutching her smarting chest, Iris looked too. She saw that the figure on the ledge had raised itself up on two legs, neither moving nor trying to hide itself. It was wearing a coat or hood, so they couldn't see its face, but Iris could feel its gaze as firmly as if she was being touched.

Lees swore. He raised the rifle again, but Floyd slapped it away. "Are you mad?" He turned to his sister in the dirt, offering her his hand. Over his shoulder she could see the fury on Lees' face, and she thought he was going to turn the gun on Floyd, or her, or both of them. She saw him look back to the ledge, and his malice disappeared, replaced by eye-flicking panic. Following his gaze, she saw that the figure that had been watching them was gone.

Floyd pulled her up. As she rose to her feet he winced,

and at the pain on his face she forgot about Lees and reached for Floyd's back. Her hand slipped off him as he looked up at the ledge. When he saw that the watching figure had disappeared he turned back to Iris, then to the pool, the forest, the peaks. Confusion came to his face, and concern—about the missing watcher, Iris assumed, but when she looked around she realized instantly her mistake. Patrick Lees had gone, too.

12

LEES HAD LEFT his horse and bag by the myrtles—all he had taken with him was his gun and waterskin. The twins checked their gear to make sure he'd not taken anything from them, even though he wouldn't have had the time. Rushing about, checking saddlebags, being busy: it helped Iris remain calm, at least outwardly. Internally she was a mess. Nothing sat straight in her head, and every few seconds she looked around the forest for Lees, and then up at the place where the watcher had been standing.

When they'd accounted for all their possessions Floyd whirled to face her. "What the damn hell was all that about?"

Iris felt blood rise to her skin. "How should I know?"

"A lot more chance of you knowing than me."

Iris held her breath, stopped herself from responding. She looked back at the river. "He can't have gone far."

"Let him, then." Floyd had untethered his horse. "I'd

rather find the fella he tried to shoot." He led it down to the pool, then up toward the rapids.

Iris hesitated. She looked at Lees' horse, waiting patiently. She wouldn't be able to lead two mounts. And he might come back for it—he'd need his tent and supplies, eventually, wherever he'd run to. Then she wondered at the way she was thinking, as if she was worried about him, as if her breast wasn't still aching where he had kicked her, where he had held her so recently, where she had directed his hand. She noticed her bridle was wobbling, so she checked her horse's mouth, trying to see what it had found to chew on, before she realized she was shaking.

She decided that she wouldn't think about any of it until she knew more, so she followed Floyd up to the ledge from where the figure had been watching them. Another pool lay here, larger than the one below but just as blue, and more tranquil. On its shore Floyd found a set of wet boot prints leading away from the water and into a grove of ferns. The trail was clear as they followed it into the grove, brushing through ferns that were small at the river's edge but grew taller the further they went, taller than the twins, taller than their horses. Iris could see that the tracks were uneven, how one boot was dragging in the loam, and as they followed them she felt tense, alert, alive. Then the drooping fronds opened up, revealing a clearing lit with bright sunbeams that slanted through a ring of the towering foliage.

In the center lay a large structure of a kind Iris had

never seen before: a single slab of material, long and wide, which rose from the forest in a spherical, grotto-like formation. Part of it curved away from the main dome and tapered down toward the earth. Where it met the ground another piece emerged from the dirt, flatter and straighter, sporting an array of dagger-like spikes that ran in two rows back toward the dome. All of it was a grayish-white color, smooth to the eye except where sections were furred by wet moss. Toward the rear of the main slab sat large holes, facing the twins at about the height of their heads, and out of one of them climbed a weak column of smoke.

The twins stared. Iris understood what she was looking at, while at the same time not making any sense of it. It was one thing to see bones surrounding an inn, or rising ghostlike from peat and plain. This was much more: too much, too alien. It took Floyd saying it out loud for her to accept the reality of it.

"It's a skull."

The boot prints led between the spikes—the teeth—and into the skull's smoking interior. Again the twins looked at each other, before Floyd tethered their horses, unsheathed his knife and began to follow the tracks, crouching as he entered the gaping mouth. After a moment, Iris followed him.

Inside they found the source of the smoke: a small pile of coals, more black than red or orange. Around it the earth had been scraped flat, and on this floor was the figure that had been watching them, half-slumped against the smooth wall of bone. It was lying beside a saddlebag made of fine leather and was wearing a long black coat.

The twins moved slowly to its side, Floyd's knife ready. They could hear uneven breathing, a rattle in the throat. When they turned it over they found that it was a man, unconscious or asleep, black-bearded and middle-aged, dirt and grime etched into the lines of his face. Hunger had sucked the flesh out of his cheeks. Dried blood snaked from his left ear.

Floyd sheathed his knife and felt the man's forehead. He stood up, stretched his back and turned to the fire, frowning at its meager light. Then he looked at Iris, who had sat down, and although they were close to each other neither of them spoke for some time.

There was a deep hollow in a portion of the skull below the unsmoking eye socket, worn there by the dripping of rain over hundreds or thousands of years. Iris filled it with fresh water that she collected from the blue pool using the small iron bucket she kept in her pack. When the hollow brimmed she dipped in a cloth, which she used to clean the unconscious man's face. He shifted at her touch, but did not wake up.

While Iris carried water and washed their host, Floyd fed strips of bark to the coals, blowing on them until they smoked and flamed. He added dry twigs, then sticks, then built a tent of fallen limbs over the fire until it crackled and burned unassisted. He left, and was gone for a while, and came back with three small fish of a species Iris had never seen before—black, whiskery, multi-finned. He slit them open, buried their guts, threaded their bodies with straight sticks and set them to cook above the flames. Iris kneaded together a ball of damper, which she rolled out and placed on a flat rock by the fire to cook.

The twins sat down, still not talking. They waited, stretched, warmed themselves by the fire. And as the skull begin to fill with smells of charring fish skin and baking bread, their unwitting host began to stir, and moan, and finally he woke up.

He hauled himself up onto his elbows, and looked first at the healthy fire. He sniffed, saw the cooking food, rubbed his eyes. He touched his face, stroking the clean skin. Then he saw the twins and stared at them for a long time, as if trying to figure out whether they were real.

Iris handed him a mug of water. He took it, drank slowly, drank long, the whole time staring at her. When at last he took his eyes away, Iris spoke.

"Are you all right?"

He didn't say anything, but took another drink before leaning over his right knee and rolling up the dirty cuff of his trouser, grimacing with pain. Beneath the torn fabric was a vary-colored knot of flesh, purple and yellow and blue, swollen to twice the size of a normal ankle. He looked down at it, then back at Iris, then into his empty mug.

She refilled it and handed it back to him. She waited for him to explain his injury but he did not, so she spoke again.

"You're the Patagonian."

At that he sat up straighter. "Is that what I'm being called?" His voice was soft, lilting, with a musical accent. "I quite like it."

"You don't sound like a Patagonian."

The stranger shrugged. "I developed my accent at school, I'm afraid. Back in the old country. Mother and Father thought I needed a proper education." He gave the twins a weak smile. "In any case, it's probably easiest if you call me Jon."

"As you wish." Iris nodded.

He looked from face to face. "I assume you have names."

Floyd leaned forward. "Floyd Renshaw. And my sister, Iris."

Jon sipped again at his water. His smile faded, and a hardness came to his expression. "But it wasn't just the two of you. Where's your partner?"

Floyd twisted one of the skewered fish. "Ran off on us. Right after he tried to shoot you." Fat dripped from the crisping skin onto the coals, sizzling and smoking on impact. "Was hoping you might be able to tell us why."

Jon exhaled. "Ah." He leaned back. Looked to the cooking fish and damper. "So you don't plan on killing me."

"No."

"What wonderful news."

He kept looking at the food, rubbing at his lips, seemingly uninterested in saying anything else.

Iris checked her damper and saw that it was mostly done. She teased it away from the fire with a stick, flipped it over a few times, then tore a doughy strip off its edge, which she used to grasp one of the fish and strip the flesh off its small bones. She handed it to Jon, who took the food eagerly but politely from her hands, nodding in thanks. Then he fell on it like a wolf.

The twins glanced at each other, but did not interrupt his meal.

When he had devoured it, Iris gave him another strip of damper filled with more of the oily fish. This one he ate more slowly, seeming to savor the taste as he licked his fingers. When he was done he wiped his face and swallowed more water, before leaning back against the skull's wall and turning his haggard gaze back onto Iris and Floyd.

"Killing is still why you're here, though. You've come for the bounty."

Floyd poked at the fire. "So have you."

A wistful look came to Jon's face. "You're correct, I suppose." He gathered himself. Sat up straighter again. "Although my price was much higher than the public bounty. Those sheep farmers offered me a small fortune to catch her. Still, I wasn't sure I wanted to accept it. I didn't need the

money, and I'd told myself that I was finished with hunting.
I am not a young man, and I stopped gaining pleasure from
besting a puma many years ago. But I reread the letter, and
I found myself thinking again and again of this poor beast,
alone at the far border of the world. I thought of the pain she
must be going through, to be hunted by fools who do not
understand her, to be hounded to the end of her days. The
last of her kind, in a place where she never belonged. It filled
me with sorrow, and I could not shake her from my mind
or my dreams. So I came all this way, across an ocean and
more, to end her misery. I felt it was the least I could do."

"Fool," muttered Floyd.

"Pardon?"

"You're a romantic fool."

Jon drank again. "You see me true." He smiled at Floyd,
then watched the fire crackle up the third skewer of fish.
"From the harbor I came straight up to these plains. I met
with some of your graziers—hungry people, although they
are fed more than well enough—and agreed to their terms.
From there I set about gathering information, and in the
process I met a young man who offered to act as my guide.
Usually I work alone, but the land was foreign to me, and
he seemed curious, not possessed with the terror and blood-
lust the rest of your people are afflicted with, so I agreed to
take him on. We moved into the mountains proper and I
began my work."

Jon seemed to be gathering energy. A propulsive

rhythm came to his speech. "As I passed through this country I saw how different it was from the glaciers of my homeland—different, yet in some ways similar. It was strange to me, and it made me wonder how strange it would seem to a puma. The sadness that had found me when I first learned of Dusk returned, stronger this time, and for the first time in my life I began to doubt that I'd be able to squeeze the trigger when I found my quarry. I considered turning back, going home, abandoning the hunt I didn't crave and the money I didn't need.

"But I had come so very far, so I decided that I would sleep on the decision. It was a clear night and I slept out under the stars, on a bed of that very green, very soft grass you have here, the grass that is like a pillow. The air was so clean, and wonderfully cold. And then it came to me: I would not kill Dusk." Color filled his hollowed face. His voice went soft. "I would bring her home with me, alive."

When he spoke these words Iris felt something cold move beneath her skin, drenching her from scalp to ankle, chilling but not unpleasant. A prickling sensation that was both numb and sharp. It was something like understanding or recognition, but she couldn't be sure.

"How?" Iris fought back into herself, breaking the silence that had filled the skull after Jon had spoken.

He reached into the folds of his coat and pulled out a small vial. "With this." He held it up to his eye, as if measuring the dark liquid inside. "One drop will paralyze a man. Three will kill him." He returned it to his pocket. "The same amount will put a puma to sleep for a day. By continuing carefully to administer it, one can keep even the largest of cats incapacitated for as long as it takes to imprison them by more conventional means."

Floyd looked up from the fire, skeptical. "You've seen it done?"

"I've done it myself." Jon shrugged. "It's an inexact science, but it works."

"But how would you get the creature down from the mountains?"

Jon smiled at him, perhaps mockingly, perhaps sadly, before he glanced down at his injured leg. "A question that no longer matters much."

The day's rain had returned, the soft kind that had come in the morning. It hazed past the eye sockets in a gentle mist.

Iris watched it glisten the fronds, then turned back to Jon. "What happened?"

He flexed his ruined ankle. "The morning after I'd made my decision I revealed my plan to my guide. I was straight with him, and said I did not expect him to go along with it—he was hoping for a cut of the bounty, of course, and there was no certainty the graziers would still pay me for removing the beast alive. But he decided to stay with

Dusk

me. He told me my plan was a grand one, noble and bold, and that surely the graziers would honor the bounty, for I was still removing Dusk and thus solving their problem."

Jon's voice stalled. He looked exhausted.

"Rest," said Iris. "You don't need to tell us everything. Not right now."

But Jon shook his head. "I'm nearly done." He sat up, gathered himself. "Together, we got to work. From interviewing those who had seen her and by examining sites where Dusk had made her kills, I began to understand her. This might make little sense to you, but to catch a puma one must know them, and I came to see that Dusk was taking human prey not out of viciousness or a particular liking for their taste, but desperation. She was being pursued so relentlessly—coarsely and without skill, but relentlessly nonetheless—by your countrymen that her hunting range had widened in response. She was being chased off her trails, forcing her to travel far further each day. It would have made her exhausted, ravenous, so when a hunter got too close she took them, as much out of annoyance as hunger." He smiled weakly. "Everyone has bad moods.

"From there, all I had to do was look at a map, mark the locations and dates of her kills, and triangulate her movements to the kind of terrain pumas like to call home. Somewhere steep, rough, protected." He stretched out a flat palm and waved it slowly through the air between them. "Here."

After a pause, he continued. "As soon as we moved upriver I began seeing signs of her, some of them fresh. I started feeling the old thrill, the danger—it was like a hunt from my youth. That I wasn't going to kill her made it all the more exciting." He scratched at his neck. "After a day of scouting I decided I would lay my trap by the water, a few hundred yards upstream from here. I shot a small kangaroo—a wallaby, I think you call them—and spread him out in a place with clear lines of sight.

"My guide was with me. He had been helpful the whole time, willing to do anything I asked. But now, with the wallaby in place, he stopped. He told me it wouldn't be enough, a little thing like this. Dusk was a man-eater, he said. Surely I understood, he said." Jon paused to study the forest outside. He shivered, as if the misting rain was hitting his skin. "Then he struck me in the throat.

"I fell into the stream and at once he was on me, holding me down. As I struggled and swallowed water I came to understand what was happening, what he was doing. Even while I was drowning I could see how terribly clever his plan was. Cruel and selfish, of course, but clever as the devil. And it was something that apparently hadn't occurred to any of the rest of you: to bait a man-eater with a freshly killed man. Into the bargain, he hadn't even needed to find Dusk's territory—I had done that for him." Jon grimaced. "It all made a horrible kind of sense.

"Down there in the water I realized that he had no intention of letting me live, so I let the last of the air leave my lungs and my body go slack. I felt myself begin to float. My chest was burning and I was sure I was dying, but still I did not move, not until I felt his hands come off me. Then I twisted away from him and did the only thing I could: I flung myself into deeper water.

"The current took me. I was gasping for air, sucking in as much as I could, and I was being tossed wildly by the river, but I could see him chasing me down the bank. If he was speaking or shouting at me I couldn't hear anything. He shot at me—with my own rifle, which he had picked up from the riverbank, no less—but he missed. The fellow is no marksman, thank god. I had no plan of escape, no idea but to get away from him.

"Then I heard a churning roar, and felt air wrap and pull my legs, and then I was falling: falling for what felt like a long time, down a waterfall I had forgotten we'd passed that morning." He chuckled. "It was a majestic sight, and we'd seen it only an hour earlier. It's amazing what the mind will so quickly forget.

"When I crashed into the base of the falls I landed half in water, half on rock." He pointed at his ankle. "That's how I gained this injury. But even with the pain it caused—and it was a great pain, one of the greatest I have felt—I knew I needed to keep moving, to hide from him. So I crawled into the trees, using my good foot to kick soil over the marks my body had made. Not long later, I saw him come looking for me.

"My trail was broad, but luckily he is as poor a tracker as he is a marksman. I watched him search for nearly an hour. He grew frustrated, and then I saw him grow scared. He started calling out my name, saying that it was an accident, that he was there to help me. Then he looked up at the height of the falls, as if reassuring himself that I couldn't have survived. I watched him leave, but I waited until the moon was fully risen to try to move again."

Jon was flagging badly now. His words were coming slow and slurred. Again Iris tried to get him to stop and rest, but he waved her off, pulled in a long breath, and continued. "I couldn't manage much, not with my injury. As you can see, I still can't. I retrieved my pack and gear—he had not thought to steal those, the cretin. Then I crawled through the trees for hours, until the sun had started to rise and I found shelter here, in this strangest of caves." His voice turned thoughtful. "A whale, I think it must have been, although not like any whale I have ever seen. It is too big, and the teeth indicate a savage predator, more ferocious than anything in our oceans. In any case . . ." He looked to Iris, his face pained, tired. "You asked me what happened. That is what happened."

*

The skull was silent, save for the light patter of the rain, although Iris had stopped hearing it. She wasn't hearing anything; her body was filling with dread and horror, a black tide of horror. Unbidden, she began to recount to Jon everything they'd seen and heard since they came up the northern passage. She told the truth, not concealing anything, trying to remember exactly what they'd been told, who had said what. Her ears felt hot, her mouth dry.

Floyd stood up and kicked at the coals, before piling more sticks onto them, fussing with their arrangement. Iris knew that he felt the need to move, to be busy, because she felt it, too; she wanted to stride outside, to check the perimeter around the clearing, to feel cool rain on her scalp.

Somehow Jon had pulled himself up and was casting about the skull, looking for something. "There must be something I can do for you two. I had some mushrooms somewhere, drying. They should help to make a fortifying broth."

Iris stared at him, stunned, not knowing what to say in response. But Floyd stood up, whirled around. His face was pale. "Why would you offer us anything?"

Jon looked surprised. "You've come to my aid. You may very well have saved my life." He bowed his head. "And you have my sympathies."

"What the hell do you mean, man? You're the one who's half-dead." Floyd's voice was loud now.

Jon sat back down. He took slow breaths, contemplated the roof of bone above them. "I have thought long and hard about why my companion believed he could kill me. Even though it suited his purpose, it is still the murder of a person, and it is not so easy to get away with murder. Or it shouldn't be. There is a rule of law in this land, and while these graziers who seem to be in charge are greedy, and cruel in ways they seem not to comprehend, they pride themselves on this rule of law. Any report of a death would be catalogued. Any murkiness in detail would be noted. If foul play were suspected, the family of the deceased would have cause to investigate. To seek the truth."

His eyes moved to Iris. She did not meet his gaze, so they settled on Floyd. "But I am a stranger in this place. I know nobody, and nobody knows me. As I lay here for days, unable to walk, it became clear to me that my guide went through with his attempt on my life for the simplest of reasons: he knew he would get away with it. There is nobody in this country who would care enough to investigate my death. If my companion came down from the mountain with Dusk's body, saying that she had killed me before he could shoot her, he would be regarded a hero. Nobody would question his story, because nobody would miss me . . . so you both have my sympathy."

He stretched his leg, wincing at the movement. "Because he must have felt the same way about you."

13

THE TWINS TOOK turns keeping watch during the night. Floyd took the first shift, sitting in the shadow of the jaw so that he had an unbroken view of the clearing. While Jon slept close to the fire, Iris found a flat space of dirt in the colder recesses of the skull. If she lay on her side she could see through the left eye socket to the darkness outside.

Clouds hung thick above the trees, but soon a high wind began dragging them away, revealing thousands of the shining stars that hung in these skies. As Iris stared up at them through the frame of bone she realized she'd been looking forward to seeing their vivid light, their streaking patterns, that in the short time she'd been in the highlands she had already come to rely on the calming comfort they gave her at the end of each day. She stared hard at them, hungering for that comfort, until she fell into a weak sleep.

When Floyd woke her she took his spot by the jaw,

sitting behind the twin rows of teeth. They didn't speak as they swapped places. They hadn't spoken since Jon had told them his story, which Iris had been thankful for—the dread and horror she'd felt when Jon revealed the truth about Patrick Lees had not left her, and she'd been unable to do much but sip her water, feeling sick. If Floyd had screamed at her she would have accepted his curses. If he had stood up and left she wouldn't have tried to stop him.

But instead he had offered to take the first shift. As she took his position she noticed that he had loaded the fire with more wood; she could feel it heating her back while the outside air chilled her face. She rubbed her hands, flexed her toes against the leather of her boots, pulled her collar tight. She reminded herself to focus on the forest, the path, not to look up at the stars.

In the unmoving night the sickening feeling that had been gripping her intensified. She thought of what Lees had done to Jon, what he'd no doubt planned on doing to her and Floyd. She remembered the times that she'd coincidentally run into him, and the friendly mystery he'd cultivated around himself in those meetings. All those little smiles that were not wary kindness, as she'd assumed, but calculations. How he'd coaxed her into coming out here with him. How she'd suspected nothing and dragged Floyd along with them.

She thought of how quickly she'd believed Lees, how

easily she'd let herself be seduced. How she'd hungered for him, without seeing the truth of who he was. How she'd gone into his tent, how he'd smiled as she'd pulled off her shirt, how he'd held her hand afterward, and what he'd said to her, his voice a murmur, so close to her ear. *I've known who you are since the moment we met.*

It was becoming hard to get air into her lungs. Her face was slick with tears and she felt close to retching. The image of Lees' little smile as he shot a red hole through Floyd's neck came to her, and she couldn't shake it from her mind, and then she was stuffing knuckles into her mouth to force down a howl.

Iris tried to distract herself by thinking of the other things Jon had told them, everything he'd done before Lees betrayed him. She tried to picture Patagonia, but she didn't know anything about it, and all that came to her mind was a grander version of the high plains, deeper rivers, steeper mountains, whiter snow, and not one lonely puma but hundreds of them, stalking the alien ranges. She thought of the trip Jon must have taken across a wild sea—unimaginable to her, other than through the stories her parents had told her of their own miserable voyage.

She thought of the melancholy he'd felt about a creature he'd never seen, of his epiphany, his impossible mission, the fiery resolve it had filled him with. She thought of the curious love that had showed itself when he spoke about taking Dusk home. She imagined him moving up into the highlands with Patrick Lees at his side, then preparing to travel back through them with a sedated puma.

It made her think of her own passage through the plains, and how the country had got inside her, had changed her. She came to see that her journey had mirrored Jon's, in company and scenery; only he knew what he was doing, whereas she and Floyd knew nothing but desperation. She saw how in this deathly beautiful place Jon had found for himself a purpose. She thought of how they had both, at very different times, dived into violent water.

A chill came to her, the same chill she'd felt when Jon had revealed his scheme to them, and with it came a sudden flash of clarity, cutting through her mind like white fire. Her breathing steadied. She felt her face and found it dry, salty, cold as a glacier.

Iris thought of skinned seals. She thought of a wolf-hound's jaws. She thought of a trapped eagle, of sprinting deer. She focused her eyes and saw that dainty snow was falling through the foliage: soft, steady, noiseless. She watched it settle in the clearing, filled with a strength of purpose she'd never felt before.

She knew what she would do next. Nothing had ever been so clear to her.

*

Floyd rose at dawn and Iris returned to her spot at the back of the skull to sleep for another hour. When she woke, Jon and Floyd were sitting in the clearing, around a new fire Floyd must have made, their breaths rising as mist. The horses were by the fire, too, nosing at each other, warming themselves. Iris thought of Lees' horse, and wondered if he'd gone back for it. He must have, she told herself. Not even he would leave a horse to the winter.

Snow lay on the ground, coated the ferns, lay in thin banks on the limbs of the taller trees. Iris approached the pair and accepted a mug of tea from her brother, who did not greet her. As she sat down she saw that they had been talking, that she had interrupted them.

Floyd was staring into the whitened forest. "Thought he'd come in the night."

Jon was chewing fresh damper. "I wouldn't worry about that. Lees is devious, but he's also a coward. He knows he's outnumbered and out of his depth. All he had were his lies. Without them, he's more or less harmless." Jon tore off another heel of bread. "He'll have got his horse and be a long way from here by now."

Floyd nodded, a slight frown on his face. "You're probably right. I don't follow his plan, though. If he came here with you earlier, why would he have needed us to guide him?"

"I imagine he needed a reason to convince you to come with him. If you didn't think he needed your help, then it wouldn't have made sense for him to share the bounty. It would've made you suspicious. And obviously he wasn't going to tell you that he planned on using you as bait." Jon swallowed. "That's one possibility. But I think the truth is simpler: he couldn't remember the way, and he needed you to find it for him."

Floyd finished his tea, threw the dregs on the snow. "Still don't see why he'd go along with it if he knew you were up here."

"He thought I had drowned." Jon was massaging his ankle. "When he saw me, he panicked and tried to finish the job."

"Then the man's an idiot."

"He fooled you."

Floyd glared at Jon.

Jon was smiling back at him. "Almost as much as he fooled me."

They began chuckling.

Iris could see how easy they'd become in each other's company, and she wondered how long Jon had been up, how long they'd spent around this little fire, what else they had talked about.

When their laughter died she cleared her throat. "We'll help you."

Finally Floyd looked at her. His face communicated nothing. He stood up, turned to Jon and nodded at his horse. "You can ride her. We'll have to go slow, but I guess that'll suit you."

Jon bowed his head and was about to speak, but Iris cut him off. "No." She was talking to Jon, but looking up at Floyd. "I mean we'll help you catch Dusk. Help you take her home."

Floyd's eyes went wide. His cheeks tensed, his body stiffened—all of him rigid, his skin washed out.

Jon was staring at her, confused. "I beg your pardon?"

"We'll help you. I will, at least."

"Why? There is nothing for you in this."

"Probably not."

Iris could feel Floyd's eyes on her, but her mind was steady, certain. She heard him take in a long breath. She thought he was going to say something, maybe even shout, but instead he stomped back into the skull. She could hear him gathering his possessions.

Jon was still studying her. "What do you want?"

Iris went to answer him, but faltered. The decision had made sense when it came to her in the night. And it still made sense—even thinking about it now calmed her—but she couldn't articulate why. She wanted to return Dusk to Patagonia for the same reasons Jon did, but there were other ones, too, more about herself.

It would be the right thing for the creature; it would also be the right thing for her and Floyd, a chance to assist in an act that went beyond their own survival. A chance to fix a wrong in the world, and in the process somehow fix a wrong within themselves. And if that was too much of a reach, at the very least she knew that doing something new would be good for them.

She knew it all in the passage of her blood, in the ticking of her gut. But she couldn't get any of it into words. Her head hurt. Her mouth was dry, her tongue too large. "I just—"

"Work." She was cut off by Floyd, who had come back out of the skull, bag in hand. "We want work. We need work. That's all we've ever needed." He moved to the horses. "There much work in Patagonia?"

Jon shrugged. "As much as there is here, I suppose. Although my family owns farms. We always need people to plow the fields, look over the herds." He raised his voice to Floyd, who was inspecting his horse's fetlocks. "Are you capable of that?"

Floyd snorted. "More than capable."

Iris nodded.

Floyd began strapping his saddle. "How can we be sure you'd hire us? We could come all the way to Patagonia only to have you drop us like hot rocks."

Jon's face had lit up. His voice went soft, serious. "If you help me do this, you will always have work. As much as you'll ever need."

Floyd lowered the fetlock he was checking, turned to face them both. Anger and frustration all over him. "How would we even do it? Even if we put her to sleep with your magic potion, how will we get her across an ocean?"

"I have a berth booked on a ship," said Jon. "I know the captain. He trusts me."

"Why should we?" Floyd spat the words. Turned back to his horse. Stared angrily into its ear.

It was quiet in the clearing again. After a minute Iris stood, moved to Floyd's side and began inspecting her own horse. Jon, having opened his mouth to respond, paused, and limped back into the skull.

Floyd rubbed his horse's flank. "This is mad." Put his fingers into its mane. "And he's right. There's nothing in this for us."

Iris pulled up a thick bottom lip. "Nothing for us anywhere." She peered at the color of her horse's teeth. "Never has been."

He stepped back. Ran his eyes up and down his horse. Iris could see that he was frustrated, uncomfortable. That he might ride off on her; this might be it for them. She saw herself alone on another continent. Saw herself torn open on a riverbank, her hot blood blooming in white water.

Floyd laughed, and kept laughing for quite some time, and he told his sister that she was a fool, and that he couldn't stand her, that she was going to get them killed, was determined to get them killed, and that they may as well die as they'd lived: together.

*

They finished packing and moved down to the blue pool, Iris leading the horses, Jon's arm slung over Floyd's shoulder. Snow bordered the water and ice rimed the rocky shore. As the horses drank Jon repeated the plan he'd told them the previous day, the one he'd been following before Lees' betrayal. His voice was both excited and firm, as if what he was telling them was of great importance. Which, Iris realized, it was. Floyd was right. They were in Dusk's territory. Death could come at any moment.

When he'd finished going over the details, Jon peered at their saddlebags and other gear, before turning to Floyd. "Where is your rifle?"

"Don't have one."

"You came hunting a puma without a rifle?"

"Sounds bad when you say it like that." Floyd said it with a barely perceptible whine—a false note of injury. Again Iris wondered how long they'd spent together around the fire.

Jon smiled. "Well, as you know, Lees took mine." He reached into his shirt and pulled out a small pistol. "But I still have this. And enough of my powder has stayed dry. I'll need to get closer than I usually would, but it should work."

He pointed to where the river flowed into the pool. "Go upstream and find the spot I have described to you. The place where the course widens, where there is a little stretch of bright sand. If you find a wallaby or possum—a young deer would be even better—try to kill it. Can you do that without a gun?"

The twins stared at him. Jon waited, and when he realized that this was their response to his question, he shrugged. "Well, however you do it, spread the body over the sand in the center of the beach, where the lines of sight are longest and broadest. Try to do it quietly—puma have remarkable hearing, and I don't recommend attracting her attention before we are ready." He looked down at his ankle, rolling it lightly. "I will follow you. I will be slow, but by the time you are done, I will be in place."

Iris looked at the rushing river. "How long will it take her to catch the scent?"

"Could be days. Could be minutes." He grinned. "Depends where she is."

Jon fished through his pocket, retrieving a round piece of shot and the vial he'd shown them the night before. He tried to uncap it while holding the pistol in his other hand, but he was unsteady on his bad ankle, and couldn't quite manage it. Floyd moved close to him and took the vial, allowing Jon to hold the shot as Floyd poured three fat, dark-shining drops onto its surface. Jon rolled the lead ball in his palm until its entire surface glimmered with poison, before popping it into the pistol's pan. He returned the gun to his pocket with care and bent down awkwardly to wash his hand in the pool, cracking through the thin surface ice, scouring his skin with the gravel of the riverbed until his palm was numb, bloodless, clean.

Then he straightened up, shaking flecks of ice from his fingers, and looked upriver, at the forest and the water and the clouded sky.

"Let's begin."

For the second time since they'd come to the highlands the twins set out into a world held still by snow. The snow concealed what paths and trails might have wound through the trees, so they stuck close to the riverbank, leading the horses by their bridles. At times this was difficult; mud and ice made them slip, and occasionally large boulders or thick roots ran into the water, which were hard to maneuver their horses over or around.

Despite these obstacles, they were still faster than Jon. At first he'd been by their side, but soon he needed to rest, and then he took a long time negotiating his body over a rotting myrtle trunk, and then he was a hundred yards in their wake. He waved to them as he leaned against a sturdy tree, urging them on. After that they could no longer see him.

The part of the river they were following was as wild as the section they'd seen the previous day, slashed white by rising stones and hurried by the countless tons of water it carried. Iris expected to be as unsettled as she'd been the day before, as she always was around rough water. To her surprise, she discovered that she was able to watch it break and fly beside her without anxiety. She didn't enjoy looking at it, and she was still in no way comfortable in its presence, but the change was undeniable. She pondered this strange strengthening of nerve for a moment, but the difficulty of their passage gave her no time to consider it further.

Above them the mountain range was close, now appearing even steeper. Iris could see its pocked textures, the cragging columns jutting out from its face, the palette of browns and charcoals and crystal that pushed out of the otherwise gray rock. Snow clung to it in rough quilts. There were few birds; the ones Iris did see were large, sharp-beaked, with jackets of black, white tail feathers and fierce yellow eyes: currawongs. They followed the twins through the morning, hopping from boulder to limb, winging through the complex patterns of branches. Waiting for something to fall their way.

At midday they reached the place Jon had told them about: a flattening of the terrain, a thinning of the forest, a widening of the river, and on its bank a small beach of quartz-white sand. The broader waterway and less-rugged surrounds opened up the world, letting in more mountain, more sky. Iris knew nothing about catching pumas, but if one wanted somewhere that offered both cover and good lines of sight, this place seemed ideal.

She and Floyd reasoned that it would be best to keep their mounts as far from Jon's trap as possible. At the last set of rapids they let the horses drink, then forced their way into the foliage until they found a stone ledge that provided shelter from snow and wind. They covered the horses with blankets and poured oats on the ground below their noses. They said goodbye, touched them on their shoulders and necks, and retraced their steps.

Back at the water they started moving around the bank to the little beach. Without horses the going was easier, especially on the flatter shore.

Iris looked up at the mountains. Felt within herself and found just enough energy. "I'm sorry."

Floyd's eyes were moving across the whitened forest. "Gotta die someday."

"Not about this." Her boots landed heavily on the snow. "About Lees."

At that Floyd stayed quiet for a while. When he spoke, his voice was even. "I'd imagine so," he said. "You sure got that wrong."

"I did."

"Couldn't have been more wrong."

"I'm aware."

"Probably make the gazette." He paused, focusing on a shadow in the trees. Kept his voice steady. "New record for how completely fucken wrong a person can be."

Iris let his words fall unanswered, let them settle between them, until their sting was gone and they were both smiling—not at each other, but smiling nonetheless.

14

BEFORE LONG THE twins arrived at the beach. The snow had not settled on the sand, which allowed the grains to squeak beneath their boots, loud and strange.

Iris took in the water, flowing fast but clear.

Floyd's eyes were still roving over the forest behind them. "Better go find that wallaby, then."

"Want a hand?"

Floyd raised an eyebrow. They both knew he would have more chance of spotting game without her, of getting close to it, hitting it with a thrown stick.

Iris rolled her eyes and turned back to the river. "Don't be all day about it."

Floyd stepped off the beach and moved into the forest. "Shouldn't take long."

*

Iris watched him meld into wood and leaf, then sat down facing the water. She felt calm: no longer twisted up, or full of loathing for herself, or pulled taut by fear. As she watched the river flow she realized that once they caught Dusk, she would leave these highlands and never return. Never see this fast water again, or the stiller waters of the tarns on the plains. Never see the soft cushion grass or tussocks of buttongrass. Never walk beneath the old trees. Never ride through fields of bones, never see currawongs dart or hear cockatoos trill. Never pass through these mountains, never sleep beneath these stars.

She thought of Patagonia, and all the wonders it surely held, and asked herself why she felt so sure that life there would be any different for her and Floyd. It would have been good to have some kind of assurance, she supposed, something more than Jon's promise of work, even though such a thing was impossible. And she would've liked to see Lydia again. Would have liked to sit by her fire, to hear her talk.

The slow tumble of her thoughts was interrupted by a short, harsh bark, bursting from the forest at her back. Loud and animal in its anguish. If Iris didn't know better she might have thought it was Dusk, marking the boundary of her territory. But she knew this noise as well as she knew her own voice. She'd heard it countless times, from across fires, through walls, over wide paddocks and up against the curl of her ear. A sound she could recognize in her sleep, a sound she could pick out in hell: the sound of Floyd's pain.

She was on her feet in a second, into the trees in another, crashing over snow and rock, through fronds and branches, flying toward him, thinking of Dusk's teeth in him, her claws tearing him open like thin hessian. After stumbling for thirty yards or so she stopped and swung her eyes around the forest, but couldn't see him. She called his name, nearly screamed it. She dashed left and found only frozen forest. Panic took her and she fought it off, called for him again, swung her neck, and then she saw him, prone on cold snow, his right hand scrabbling at his lower back.

Air rushed out of her. She slowed down. Floyd was in agony, but there was no cat in sight; he'd had a back spasm. She moved over to him, taking off her gloves, getting ready to help him up. But at the soft crunch of her boots on the snow, his neck twisted wildly to the left, and his arm waved with more force. Iris paused, giving him space. She leaned down. Heard her brother grunt out a word—"No"—in the moment before a large shape rushed into her periphery and slammed into her temple, sending stars into her eyes, sending her sprawling.

Iris rolled, clutching her head. She tried to kneel but was

yanked by her coat back to the ground. She was hit again, this time on the jaw, a heavy blow that cracked her teeth together, trapping her tongue. Blood swamped her mouth. She was hit again and again, always on the head, until there was a pause and she felt something cannon into her stomach, winding her.

As she opened her mouth to suck in air she was grabbed around the throat, two big hands squeezing hard, a relentless pressure that bulged her eyes open, and finally she could see the hairy wrists connected to the hands that were killing her, and the long arms behind them, and beyond them the face of Patrick Lees, showing her his small smile.

Her mind burst with pain, with pressure, yet she felt herself come alight with rage. She swung her fists, clawed at his forearms and neck, scratching and hitting. But he had over a hand's reach on her, and he would not relent, and he would not stop smiling. Her face reddened and her mind went black. When her arms went limp he threw her onto the snow and turned back to Floyd, who had fought his way onto his knees.

As Iris gasped on the ground she saw Lees contemplate her brother struggling up, before launching a vicious kick into the side of Floyd's torso. Iris heard a rib snap wetly as he collapsed, even as she fought to bring air down her burning throat.

Lees turned to the sound of her gasping. "Has he

always been like this?" He kicked Floyd again, this time in the head. "I knew he was a cripple, but I didn't imagine he was so fragile."

Floyd had gone very still. Blood was leaking from his lip and each of his wheezing breaths held a sharp rattle.

Iris felt at her face, felt the smear of her own blood. Managed to bring in just enough air to speak. "I'm going to gut you."

Lees' smile was replaced by a look of thoughtfulness. "That's not a bad idea." He pulled a hunting knife from his belt. "Get the scent around."

He looked back at Floyd, checked that he still wasn't moving. Then he came toward Iris. She tried to kick at him, to fend him off, but he swatted her legs and arms away, and struck her again in the mouth, the hardest blow he'd given her yet. Her head flew back and the world began tilting. He grabbed her by the collar and began dragging her across the ground.

"Come on. We'll do this by the river." He yanked her over a fallen limb, scraping her face against hard wood. "That foreigner's an expert, after all."

By the time they made it to the beach Iris had hit her head on two rocks and been cut on her face and hands by a number of sticks, but the pain wasn't registering above her other wounds. One of her eyes had closed over. She barely saw the sand until she crashed into it.

Lees flipped her onto her back and leaned over her.

Iris drew in a ragged breath. "You were always going to do this."

He put down his knife, began pulling at her coat. "Always."

"Why?" The sand was sticking to her wounds, gritting on her face.

"Because I can." He straightened up and looked at her. Properly looked at her. "Because I should. Dusk is killing innocent people." His voice was solemn, as if the responsibility was difficult yet necessary. "And you and your brother are nothing like innocent."

The seriousness in his tone made Iris want to laugh, but she was in too much pain, and she was too scared.

Lees opened her coat and was ripping at the buttons of her shirt, and all of Iris's fury was gone; she felt only awful, consuming fear. She pawed at his hands but he slapped them away. Once her shirt was flapping open he gripped her woolen singlet and ripped it, exposing her breasts, the pale shape of her stomach.

"No." She was mumbling through swollen lips, through a mouthful of hot blood. "No, no."

Lees picked up the knife. Again he showed her his little smile. "If you scream loud enough, she'll come for you quicker."

He raised the blade, holding her down with his other hand.

Iris could see gray clouds, and to her left the white

glint of a peak. She could feel the sand squeaking beneath her struggling flesh. She could hear the river coursing behind her. From a distance she heard the choked horror of her sobs. And then she heard Lees yelp, and felt his hand come off her.

Iris squirmed away from him. Lees was standing up straight now, clutching at the trouser of his right leg, which had been torn open. "You little cunt of a man," he was saying, and he was saying it to Floyd, who was on all fours near Lees' feet, his own small knife clutched in his hand.

Lees stepped away and bent to inspect his calf. "You've barely scratched me." He rose and once more swung his boot into Floyd's side, crumpling him into the sand. The anger on his face morphed into a look of satisfaction. "At least you've saved me dragging you down here as well."

Iris twisted her neck to look at her brother. Floyd had dropped his knife and was gasping, shaking. His eyes were closed and blood was everywhere. Without thought she reached for him. Lees stood over them, the rifle long on his back, the hunting knife huge in his hand. Iris found Floyd's hand. Found something hard in his palm.

"What . . ." Lees' voice was confused, slightly slurred.

Iris looked up and saw him still above them, but wavering. Sweat was blinking up all over his face. He dropped his knife and began pawing at his brow, his neck. He staggered away from the twins, pulling at his coat. Iris watched him yank and tear at the material, his wobbling stride becoming a crazed lurch. Then his knees collapsed and he crashed into the shallows as if shot.

She didn't move. Kept watching him for a minute, two minutes, three. She waited until she was sure he was going to stay still before she turned back to Floyd, whose eyes had opened, as had the hand Iris had been trying to hold. She looked at it, remembering the hardness she'd felt, and saw in his palm an opened vial, leaking a glossy liquid that shined dark on his skin.

They lay on the sand for a long while. When they managed to haul themselves up, the first thing they did was stagger to the river and scrub their hands with icy gravel, just as Jon had done that morning when he'd handled the poison. Floyd retrieved his knife and did the same with its blade. Then they crawled a few yards upstream and drank straight from the river, long and slow. After that they tried to wash the blood from their necks and faces, but moving that much was painful, and the water's chill intensified the sting of their wounds, so they stopped. They sat back down on the beach. They tried to breathe.

Iris was focusing on getting air into her lungs, not taking in much of the world or what had happened to them. When the shock began ebbing out of her she started seeing the river again, and hearing the soft sobs coming from Floyd.

She looked over. His face was in his hands and he was trembling. Tears were streaming through his fingers, mingled with the blood of his wounds, dropping and staining the sand. Iris leaned over, wincing at the movement, and laid a hand on his shoulder.

After a while he stopped crying and straightened up, his broken face shining. "I thought I was too late. That he'd . . ."

Iris's voice came out as a rattle. "You didn't let him."

Floyd exhaled. Worked on getting his breathing under control. "Let him sneak up on me, though."

"I wasn't going to mention that."

They didn't talk for a while after that. Floyd's hand went to the part of his side where Lees had kicked him, and Iris remembered the sickening sound of a rib snapping.

"How bad?"

Floyd grimaced as he touched his shirt. "A light tickle." He looked to Iris, running his eyes over her injuries. "You?"

She felt at the mess of gashes and lumps on her face, at the closed mound of her eye, at the great flowering of bruises on her neck. "Got a pebble in my boot."

Floyd smiled, but kept staring at her injuries. Soon he began trembling again. He sucked in a deep breath, still clutching his side. Then he looked down the beach at the great dark lump that was Patrick Lees.

"Guess we won't need that wallaby."

Iris followed his gaze, but found that she couldn't look at Lees' body for more than a second. His face as he'd been strangling her flashed into her thoughts, his hands as they'd ripped open her singlet, as they'd held her in his tent. Iris felt that she was going to scream, despite the agony of her throat, scream and faint and perhaps not wake up, which would be fine, she thought: to sleep for as long as it took to forget every memory of the man, of everything he'd said and everything he'd done.

She took her eyes back to the forest and its silent snow. "When do you reckon Jon will get here?"

"Can't be far off."

Iris nodded, thinking of Jon's ruined ankle. Then terror ripped through her. "Unless Lees went for him first."

Floyd's face paled. He climbed to his feet, swaying and wincing. "I'll go have a look."

"No." Iris stood up. "You're hurt worse. I'll go."

But Floyd was already staggering down the beach. Iris took off after him, yet he was moving surprisingly fast, and she was still finding it hard to breathe. She paused, bent over, took smaller breaths.

"Won't be long," Floyd called over his shoulder.

When Iris looked up again, he was closer to the trees, almost in the forest. He turned back to her, waving his arm, motioning for her to sit down. "Rest," he shouted.

She was annoyed, but she couldn't stop him, so she

lowered herself back to the sand. Floyd began to turn back around. Mid-swivel, he paused, froze.

Iris frowned, wondering what he was doing. She called out, but he didn't look at her; he kept his eyes on the trees and raised his arm in her direction, a flat palm, although she didn't know what it meant. Then she looked to the part of the forest that had captured his attention and went as still as he was.

She was crouched on a boulder, right on the tree line. Large and bulky with power, even as she held herself in a tense crouch. A light brown coat of glossy fur. A long unmoving tail. Small rounded ears. A white mouth, bristling with whiskers. A dark nose and darker shadows around a pair of huge eyes that were green-gold, that were mesmerizing, that were locked on to Iris.

There was more to Dusk than this—a sublime beauty about her, both primal and serene—but Iris wasn't able to take it in, because the moment her eyes met the puma's Dusk exploded off the rock in a flurry of limbs, moving fast and sure, moving like water. The long muscles in her body stretching and bulging in each enormous stride. Sand bursting from the force of her sprint.

She leaped, revealing creamy belly fur, showing unsheathed claws in paws the size of skillets, and Iris raised her arms in defense, although she may as well have kept them at her side. Dusk's body smashed her backward, and her head smacked into the beach, and the hot foul steam of the puma's breath smothered her face and senses, and all she could manage was to open her good eye and see the pink tongue and black lips and massive yellow canines of Dusk's gaping jaw, and then feel them clamp onto her tender neck with a pressure that made Lees' hands seem like a game, and somewhere in the wild shock of her death she dimly realized that she had been right when she'd imagined it. So fast: it was all happening so fast.

So fast, so awfully fast—Iris had dived into the flooded stream before Floyd could move, before he could speak. He was calming her down, helping her to see why they had to stay where they were, and then she was in the water, thrashing through white waves, stroking toward their parents.

He knew she couldn't swim well, because he couldn't—nobody had ever taught them. But as with so many things, what Iris lacked in knowledge she made up for in determination. Their mother and father had become lodged in a deep pool near the middle of the stream, and Iris was already halfway to them.

Floyd yelled at her to come back, but she either couldn't hear him or was choosing to ignore him. She kept on, her arms tearing through the water, her feet kicking like they were steam-powered, her face smacked again and again by hard water but always staying above it. She was stronger than the current. She was nearly there.

Then a monstrous wave rose and broke over the rapids, swamping all three of them. Floyd felt himself snap still. He stopped yelling. When Iris emerged she was still moving fast, no longer against the water but with it, flying loosely downstream.

Floyd couldn't see their parents, wasn't looking for them: he had eyes only for his sister. He sprinted down the bank, yelling that he was coming, but all he could do was follow her passage down the torn water. He ran and ran, his body filling with the awful idea that he couldn't help her, that she was drowned already, until Iris's tumbling body slammed into a huge rock not far from the bank.

He let out a shout of relief. Then he saw that rather than resting on the rock she was being bashed against it by the relentless force of the waves, and was struggling to keep her mouth above water. Blood left Floyd's face, his legs found a new gear, and then he was scrabbling down the bank and launching himself onto the rock Iris was pinned to.

He lay atop it on his belly and flung an arm down toward her, screaming her name into the crashing torrent. It took her a while to hear him, and after she did it took even longer for her to orient herself. Finally she twisted her body so that her chest was facing the rock, tilted her neck and was able to see him. She reached for his hand, but was knocked back underwater by a flushing wave. When she came up she tried again, but couldn't reach.

Floyd's panic was rising, his voice breaking. He wiggled as far down the rock as possible without falling in. Again Iris reached, again she came up short, again she went underwater. He could see how little energy was left in her. How she wasn't so much fighting the current as being pummeled by it. Then a big wave roared into her, cracking her against the wall of stone, hard and vicious but large enough to swell her body upward, just far enough for Floyd to reach and grab her cold flailing wrist.

He began pulling her up, but the wave washed away

and her weight doubled, dragging him down toward the stream. He used his free arm to brace himself, but couldn't gain any leverage. He kicked his legs about, trying to find a foothold, trying to secure himself. The rock had been worn smooth by the stream, and there was nothing there for him. She swung heavy in his grip, a dead weight of sodden skin and flannel.

Floyd held on. He tried pulling, but couldn't raise her any higher. He began frantically strategizing, thinking of using different angles, of anything that might help. She became heavier in his hand. He could see her mouth gurgling with each flush of the current. Her eyes were mostly closed now. She had stopped making any noise.

And he came to see that there was no way around it, there was no second option, there was only one unavoidable truth: he would pull her up, or she would drown.

Floyd took in a breath. He clenched his teeth, closed his eyes and began to pull. Iris didn't move. His arm began to strain, but still she didn't budge. He let his body slacken and tried again. This time his arm hurt even more, every fiber in it, but she began to rise. He was panting and groaning, yet up she kept coming. The pain was spreading but he ignored it, even as it pushed into his shoulder, his neck. *She's going to drown*, he told himself, *she's going to die if you stop.*

He kept dragging her, feeling her limp body scrape against the rock, feeling the ache move down his collarbone. He was sure he'd snapped a tendon or pulled his bicep off its bone, but he kept pulling, and she kept coming. When her head appeared over the lip of the rock he could feel a wobbling weakness flare through his joints, so he swiveled around, planted his feet and tried to finish the job in one sudden, violent tug.

It worked. Iris's body lurched up out of the water and slapped onto flat rock. And in that vicious pull, in that new position, Floyd felt the pain fly from his arm to the base of his spine. He felt it rip and twist and explode with a new kind of pain, one that shot lightning through him.

He collapsed beside his sister, unable to move, sweating and wheezing, thanking spirits and gods for letting him save her, assuming they'd both recover, not knowing that he was wrong—that while she would regain her strength, he would not. His back would remain like this for as long as he lived: wrenched, misaligned, agonizing. A price, had he known it before he began pulling, that he would have paid without hesitation. Would've done it gladly, every day of his life. Would've cut the spine from his skin if it meant she came out of the stream breathing.

With each winter the rent discs and muscles of his lower back tightened further, solidifying into their unnatural bulge, worsened by two things that life gave him no chance to avoid: hard work and cold weather. But even through the cruellest of his pains, he never regretted its cause. He only regretted that he hadn't been as selfless as Iris. He regretted how he'd decided instantly to let their parents drown. He was glad to be rid of them and did not miss them for one second, but he wished that he'd shown an instinct for compassion. He wished he was more like his sister.

He'd thought that as soon as they were free of their parents, their lives would become easier. He'd also thought that it would be his responsibility to care for Iris—that she would need him, that he would be her protector. But while they no longer had to suffer their parents' harsh regime and violent whims, neither did they possess their guile, their knowledge, their nose for survival. And it quickly turned out that Floyd's skills—his ability to read the land, to follow tracks, to notice things—were far less useful than Iris's talents. He marveled at how she could weather cruel treatment and hungry weeks and doggedly keep going, always convinced better times were just around the corner. How she could wring work out of people who hated them on sight. How she could meet malice with a smile, bow her head, and become ever more determined.

And while he never learned how to talk about it, he saw it all, he felt it all—everything she did for them without ever asking him to pull his weight. For years he waited for her to come to her senses and abandon him, but she never did. She stayed with him, and as his back got worse, she got even better at helping him. She came to be able to see when Floyd was hurting, no matter how hard he tried to hide it from her. She learned how to knead the agony out of his back without him ever asking her to. She weathered the storm of him, whenever the pain became too much. She reeled him back from the brink, again and again, whenever he felt he had become too much of a burden for her and tried to march off into the trees.

Sometimes he watched her ride with dulled awe. Some nights he imagined life without her, and felt anxious tears sting him into sleep. Some days he lashed out at her; some days he wouldn't speak to her. Through all the months and years she remained indefatigable, optimistic and most of all kind, even though kindness had never really worked out for them. And as time passed Floyd came to see that the great gift of his life was that he spent it riding by her side, and that the troubles they faced were worth it, and would always be worth it, if you had a sister like Iris.

This didn't mean that he never grew frustrated with her, or that her patience for him was limitless—they still disagreed, still felt tension. Never more so than when they climbed up into the highlands. Floyd knew they needed work, knew they were running out of options. Knew that he could track Dusk if he had to. But he didn't want to, and tried to head Iris off as much as he could, for the most obvious of reasons: it was dangerous, and they didn't know what they were doing, and he did not want her to die.

He thought that, for once, her determination would eventually run out, and he'd be able to convince her to head back to the lowlands. But he didn't count on the land itself. As soon as they arrived on that first rocky plain, Floyd saw what was happening to his sister. How much the landscape was moving her. He realized before she did that she was feeling a deep, beyond-human connection. And in the presence of this unfurling of her love, he couldn't help but feel something similar.

This sort of thing didn't come naturally to him. His mistrusting, pain-riddled disposition left little room for optimism, and he'd known for a long time that they'd never find a place that would welcome them. Yet as they moved through the highlands, he saw how Iris was coming around to the idea that this was that place. He could read her thoughts in the shape of her face: that they would be able to build a life here, full of work, free of hatred and distrust.

He didn't agree with her, but as they pushed into the mountains her passion began to infect him. He started seeing the broader colors of the skies, the stark beauty in the emptiness of the plains. The fresh oceans of air and harsh light of the stars eroded his suspicions, weakened his gloom. It wasn't that he came to love it the way Iris did—he loved it *because* she did, which made him happier than the highlands ever made her.

In Patrick Lees he read a slyness and an arrogance that he could not trust, not for a second. But he was angry with Iris for going to the peat cutters without him, and she was mad at him for drinking with Lyle Horton, and he couldn't find a way to bring it up with her. The whole thing was infuriating to him—their pursuit of Dusk, her blindness to Lees' false charms. But Floyd had only assumed Lees would try to dupe them out of the bounty; he never imagined how sinister was his actual plan.

When Lees' betrayal was revealed, he felt no real anger at Iris about it, only relief that she was all right—that they'd escaped before Lees had gone through with his plan. And that relief didn't compare at all to what he felt when he managed to snag his knife in Lees' shin, when he watched the big bastard collapse into the water.

On the river beach, choked by new kinds of pain, all manner of rages and sorrows, he didn't think much at all. He was just happy they'd survived, so he forgot all about the highlands, the plains, the life they might have there. He forgot about almost everything, including the one thing he'd ever been good at, his one use to Iris—his ability to notice things.

*

As Dusk had flown across the sand toward her, the world slowed down. A distilled terror drenched his broken body; he couldn't watch what was happening, and neither could he look away. He felt he was coming to an end of all things, not merely in his life but in the life of the universe, for without Iris there was nothing—no reality that held him alive and not her.

He stumbled forward, yelling, screaming. He prepared to throw himself at the great cat, even though he knew Iris was already dead; he would wrestle Dusk off his sister's body and with any luck she would do him the favor of killing him, too, and save him the trouble of doing it himself.

While the beast pressed the life out of Iris he readied his calves, bent his knees. Then a shot sounded across the water. Dusk flinched, and a high yowl tore from her mouth. She lifted her red maw from Iris's neck, turned, saw Floyd and ran past him. He watched her fly toward the trees, toward Jon, who was stumbling out of the forest, his little pistol hanging weakly in his grasp.

Floyd didn't see what happened next, because he had turned back to his sister and fallen to her side, grabbing her hand, touching her face, pressing on her massive wounds as if trying to sweep all the blood back inside her, demanding that she wake up, begging her to stay with him, listening for a breath that would not come: thinking that she needed to keep breathing, that she must keep breathing, that if only she would keep breathing then he could, too.

15

ALL AROUND WAS pure darkness, a black void that sucked and pulled, that dizzied and unsteadied. Then a haze of forest green slowly crept in at the edges of this darkness. In the center of the void white lights began to flash, harsh and violent—burning minerals, bursting stars. They brought with them shock and noise and sharpness, and the only way to avoid them was to crawl out of their reach, to swim through their explosions, to come back to life.

Iris opened her eyes to a stony roof that, she began to realize, was not stone at all. She was in the skull of an ancient whale, staring up at mossy bone. Through the distant eye socket was gray light: a clouded dawn. She could vaguely recognize that she was cold, perhaps dangerously cold, but her body was pulsing with hot pain, especially her neck, all of her neck—on her broken skin and in the fibers of her muscles, in the joints of her spine and in the swollen closure of her throat. Every agonizing inch of it felt ruined.

But stronger than her pain was her thirst. Her mouth felt like it had been scrubbed with sand. She dimly remembered the hollow of bone she'd once filled with river water. She flexed her fingers. She bent a wrist. With effort she pushed herself up onto an elbow. With stiff slowness she turned her body toward where she thought the little pool might be. She thought she could see it—early sun catching a bit of shine. But between her space on the soil and the socket was a large, lumpen shape. Someone had brought a boulder into the skull, she thought, perhaps as a barrier against the wind. It made little sense, but the need for water overwhelmed any other thought that came to her.

She started to haul herself onto her knees, gritting her teeth against the ache of it. Once she'd done that, she stopped to catch her broken breath. Then she began crawling, each shuffle shooting pain into her joints, the soft dirt like sharp rocks beneath her palms. Inch by inch she closed in on the pool. Her body answered the thought of it: her mouth moistened, her thirst intensified. Determination tightened her limbs.

It was odd—the lumpen boulder was moving. Its center was rising and falling in a slow rhythm. A steady huffing noise was coming from it, too, and a smell: deep, meaty, warm. Iris paused, distracted from her thirst. She began to see that the boulder's contours were not hard and rocky but soft, smooth.

She flailed closer. The smell hit her harder, and in a

red instant she recognized it. She remembered how it had swamped her senses, the great weight on her chest and the pressure on her neck, the jaws clamping off her thread to life—and then she was falling back, and through her desert-dry throat she was shouting, she was screaming.

A figure rushed in, holding a burning stick and speaking in a soothing coo. But she was not listening; she was not interested in this figure. The glowing branch had thrown color into the skull, showing her what she had already known, and she had no eyes or thoughts for anything but the body of Dusk, lying huge and peaceful beside her, coat shining in the light.

At the sound of her rasping cries Jon stumbled into the skull, trying to help Floyd calm Iris down. But there was no doing it, not while she was so close to the puma. In the end they carried her out into the cold, sitting her beside their fire, her face to the coals. There they lay a thick blanket over her legs and brought her mug after mug of cold water. When her drinking slowed they fed her tiny slivers of fish, one oily piece at a time.

Floyd kept asking her if she was all right, but Iris kept forcing herself to drink, to chew, even though it caused her great pain. He draped his coat over her shoulders and limped about the camp, gathering more wood, laying more branches on the already healthy fire. The flames kicked high. When they had grown so tall they were licking the lowest fronds of the overhanging tree ferns, Iris managed to speak.

"Can either of you," she croaked, "make this make sense."

Jon sat back, giving space for Floyd to answer. But no words came from him.

Iris was staring at them both, confused and haggard, and under her angry gaze Floyd had split open. Tears were rivering out of his eyes, and his lips were tight and bloodless. He had reached out a hand and placed it on her boot, squeezing the hard leather over her toes, not looking at her, shaking with feeling.

It was left to Jon to do the explaining. He told her how he had arrived at the beach in time to see Dusk pounce. How he'd fired his toxic bullet into the meat of Dusk's shoulder, and how she had turned and rushed toward him, only to collapse into sleep at his feet. He told Iris how lucky she was to have such a thin neck—Dusk's jaws were so large, her canines had wrapped all the way around Iris's throat, not puncturing her flesh. Only the eyeteeth and molars had cut into her, and they were used for crushing air out of prey, not bleeding them to death. Jon's bullet had caught Dusk seconds before Iris was throttled, although the damage was great. He and Floyd had thought her dead on the sand, and were shocked to find breaths still leaking out of her.

He told Iris how they had carried her to the horses, lain her over her mount, slowly led her back to the skull. He and Floyd had spoken about the possibility of her survival—a brutal conversation, because they both knew she had little chance; all they could do was tend to her, keep her safe and dry, and hope that she held on.

It wasn't as hard to talk about as their next decision: what to do with Dusk. Floyd had wanted to leave her on the beach. Or, if they went back, to kill her. But with patience Jon wore Floyd down, convincing him that what Dusk had done to Iris didn't change the facts of his mission—their mission. Floyd had scowled, spat, disagreed. If a cat nearly killed your sister I imagine you would feel differently, he had shouted at Jon. Jon reminded him that keeping Dusk alive was what Iris had wanted.

It was only when Iris showed signs of strength—steadier breathing, steadier pulse—that Floyd relented. He agreed to go to the beach with Jon to see if Dusk lived, but promised no more than that.

When they got there they saw that the body of Patrick Lees had gone, no doubt washed away by the river, which annoyed Jon, who had hoped to retrieve his rifle. They found Dusk, asleep on the sand but beginning to stir. Floyd reached for his knife, but Jon beat him to it by shaking a drop of poison onto Dusk's fat tongue. She went still again, and Floyd turned to Jon, asking what the backup plan was, that she weighed more than the two of them combined, never mind their injuries, and what the hell did he intend to do with her.

To which Jon had smiled, and told him that he had made many mistakes, but that he was at last in the realm of his knowledge. He told Floyd what they would do, and they did it, and Floyd was furious to discover that it worked—that a sled built out of branches and slabs of bark would take Dusk's weight after they agonizingly heaved her great bulk onto it, and that two horses would be able to drag it across the beach and down the forested riverbank, all the way to their camp.

For half a day Dusk had lain by their fire, breathing softly, sleeping dreamlessly. And then it had begun to snow, and they had little choice but to drag her into the skull, beside Iris. Jon had promised Floyd that Dusk would be asleep for at least two more days, maybe more. He had promised that he'd check constantly on her. They took turns sitting with them both. It was on Jon's shift, as he'd stepped outside to stretch his ankle, that Iris had woken up.

Jon stopped talking. Let his words and the fire and the late-winter air fill the space between them. Floyd's eyes were still on the ground, but he was no longer shaking. Iris looked between them. She waited for more, yet neither of them spoke. They seemed to be waiting for her to say something.

But she had no energy to react—it was all she could manage just to sit up. She swallowed more water. Looked down at Floyd's hand on her boot. Looked over at Jon.

"You were wrong," she rasped, "about Lees."

The placid expression he'd been wearing fell away. "I'm sorry." Wincing guilt spread over his face.

He was going to say more, but Iris waved a hand at him. Tried to smile. "So was I."

He smiled back, but the guilt remained on his face.

Iris glanced around the clearing. "What now?"

Jon lifted his palms to the fire. "Well, it depends if you've changed your mind. I'd understand if you have." He cocked his head toward the skull. "But if not, then we do as we discussed. We take her home."

Iris leaned back on her sore hands. She let herself be warmed by the food and the flames. She thought about what Jon had told her, what he and Floyd had done, and although she felt gratitude and dulled wonder, she mostly felt the sting and throb of her wounds. Every part of her head ached.

What she didn't feel, she realized, was anger. She thought of Dusk, lying comatose behind them. She lifted a hand to the scabbed and mottled destruction of her neck, and tried to remember the attack. Iris tried to interrogate her thoughts, and through her pain and exhaustion and the lingering pulses of fear, she found that she felt the same way she had that night outside the skull, under the stars, cold and sure.

Her ruined neck, Jon's smashed ankle, Floyd's broken rib and wrecked back: combined, the intact bits of them would nearly constitute a properly functioning person. Their injuries would've made their passage down the sloping forest difficult even if they weren't transporting an unconscious puma. With Dusk in tow, their pace was glacial. Burdened by their wounds and weights, they helped each other over even the smallest barriers, pausing to rest whenever they needed to.

Every hour they swapped the horse that was dragging Dusk, although neither of them seemed too troubled by the load—gravity was doing a lot of the work. The sled thumped down the riverbank, sliding over roots, crashing into boulders, snapping off branches. Each time it was hauled over a rock or log or gully the twins stopped and stared at the great cat, full of fear, waiting for her green-gold eyes to snap open.

Yet she did not stir, even at the heaviest of knocks. By late afternoon they had made it to the peak of the high falls, and as the orange sun bit into the horizon they reached the confluence of the dark and pale rivers.

Their day ended on the grassy bank where the waters mixed, far enough away from where the twins had camped with Lees for Iris to be able to relax. Jon checked on Dusk, shaking another drop of poison into her mouth. Floyd and Iris built a fire, made damper, boiled water.

Iris was going to put up her tent but was too tired, so she sat down by the flames and waited for the stars to blink to life. She considered sleeping beneath them. Wondered if her weakened body could weather the night's cold.

Jon began setting up his tent—an archaic-seeming design Iris did not recognize, a pentagonal shape built with creamy cloth and elastic wooden frames.

Floyd was seeing to both of the horses. Brushing them, watering them, feeding them, checking their hooves, picking pieces of forest from their coats, laying their blankets over them. He looked exhausted, but afterward he put up his own tent. Then he hovered by Iris, studying her out of the corner of his eyes. He took off his coat and lay it on the ground beside her, then he took her tent out of her saddlebag and began assembling it beside his own.

"Would you stop bloody fussing." Her voice snapped through the twilight. "I nearly got us done in by that bastard. She"—Iris pointed at Dusk—"just about killed me. You can barely walk and I can barely breathe. Chances are, we aren't going to properly recover. But we're alive, and for better or worse we're going to stay that way." She threw a twig at him. "So give all this tiptoeing around a goddamned rest, and make us all some tea."

The camp went quiet. Night hadn't yet fallen, but it was dim enough for Iris not to be able to see Floyd's face. Then she heard laughter—Jon's laughter. She looked over the fire to see him grinning, massaging his ankle, shaking his head. Floyd limped over and sat down, and she saw that he was also grinning, and she realized that she was, too.

Floyd swung their little kettle onto its flimsy tripod. Soon it was boiling. He poured in the leaves, he let it steep, he portioned out their tea, handed around the mugs, and with bitter steam rising to her cheeks Iris finally felt herself relax.

They ate, drank, Iris tentative with the tea's heat. They fed the fire and watched the stars reveal their glow. Among them the moon was a clean half-disc, shining not white but silver. Jon and Floyd were talking, but Iris wasn't paying attention. They sounded familiar, jocular—like they had known each other for years.

Iris let the rhythm of their talk wash over her, noting how it paired with the deep rumble of Dusk's slow-pumping lungs. She stretched her arms, her legs. Then she stood, said goodnight and left them to each other. She retrieved her tent, walked into the night and set it up a good distance away from the fire, back toward the roaring falls.

The next day they didn't enter the forest the twins had come through on their way up to the confluence, but stuck instead to the course of the dark river, traveling over a buttongrass plain. The flatness of the land made their slow passage easier. They were able to walk steadily, not having to negotiate obstacles larger than a wet ditch or a mound of grass. Little snow was left on the ground. Shallow rivulets fed the river from pools of water lying in the sedges. Tall ranges at their back, lower ones to the south. Lonely trees. The occasional bone, curving up from the earth.

They kept swapping the horses, and rested whenever they needed to. After one of these stops Iris found herself walking behind Dusk's rickety sled. For the first time since the attack she was able to study the puma, to really see her. The rounded shape of her head, the broad splay of her paws, the brown coat giving way to white, the black markings around the eyes, the thick wires of whiskers: Dusk was gorgeous, intimidating even while unconscious, and unlike any creature Iris had ever seen. Yet she was also just an animal, and a sleeping one at that. Iris watched her slumber, watched her bump along, and felt a strange sense of responsibility for her, even as she struggled to breathe through her ravaged throat.

While she was taking in Dusk, Jon was telling Floyd about Patagonia. Iris overheard bits and pieces throughout the morning. She heard about cold tablelands and the razor winds that whistled through them. Dry snow on high mountains, herds of nimble guanaco that skipped over rocky ledges beneath the glint of ancient glaciers. She heard of weathered gauchos who could read the mood of the country in the movement of its grasses and the bruising of its sky. When Jon described the great rivers that were both the country's borders and its veins, his voice was full of wistfulness, passion. Now and again Floyd would murmur something in response.

At midday they stopped for lunch. Jon inspected Dusk, and once again placed a glossy drop into her mouth.

Iris saw how steeply he tipped his little vial. "You're running out."

Jon nodded. "She's uncommonly strong. And she seems to be building a resistance to the poison. Keeping her unconscious requires more of this than it would for most of her kind."

Floyd had wandered over. "Do you have enough to keep her out until we reach the coast?"

Jon shook his head. "No." He shrugged. "But I never would have."

Iris stared at him. "I take it there's a plan."

He laid a hand on Dusk's rising flank. "Of course there's a plan."

Later in the afternoon Iris began to feel a sense of recognition, although it took her a while to understand its source. The buttongrass had darkened in color, and the water it held no longer seeped beneath it but had spread into visible tarns. It looked, she realized, like peat. They started seeing white -gray trees whose branches held spiraling, celery-like leaves. Then they were coming around a bend in the river, and there was a familiar clutch of small houses, smoke rising from their chimneys, and Iris felt both delighted and foolish. She should have known Jon would come back this way; she should have remembered where this river was flowing.

Lydia met them at the entrance to the village. Her arms were crossed and her boots were muddy. It looked like she had just returned from the peat bog. The sight of her filled Iris with relief, pleasure, a rare happiness. Rather than greet them, Lydia walked past to look at their horses. Her face was inscrutable, but when she saw Dusk on the sled her eyebrows lifted.

She glanced at Jon. "Didn't think you'd manage it."

He gave a tired smile. "Had some help." He indicated the twins. "Though not the help I'd planned on."

Lydia's eyes finally met Iris's, and a small grin came to her face. "I can see."

Iris's muscles relaxed, and she smiled back.

Jon introduced them all to each other, which amused both Iris and Lydia, although they didn't say anything.

They moved into the village, where the peat cutters began to emerge from their homes, staring at Dusk. Some of them approached Lydia, questions on their faces, but Jon had shuffled to her side and beat them to it. "Can I still count on you for that commission we discussed?"

She nodded at the cutters, who turned and started toward one of the barns where they stored peat. "Let's see."

Soon the cutters returned, pulling a wagon. A sturdy timber frame rose around its side, and a heavy door was attached to the back. It looked incomplete—there were gaps in the planks, and there was no roof—and as it rolled toward them Iris could see how recent the work on it was, the fresh splinters, the blond color of the worked wood. It was a cage, she realized. A half-finished transportable cage.

Lydia looked at it. Looked at Dusk, looked at Jon. "Should be ready by morning."

Jon's shoulders slumped with relief. "Thank god."

*

The cutters took the wagon back to the barn, and through the rest of the afternoon Iris could hear them working: sawing, hammering, chiseling. The fragrant spice of cut wood filled the air.

They rested by the river. Iris wanted to speak with Lydia, but she was moving about the street, talking with people, evidently busy. The day gave way to a surprisingly mild evening, and the members of the village who weren't working on the caged wagon decided to have their dinner outside. They set about building a fire large enough to cook food for the whole community. The twins helped where they could, but nobody allowed them to do much. The cutters who had worked with Iris remembered her, and were kind, but did not ask her many questions. Mostly they wanted to watch Dusk sleep.

Jon was evidently thrilled with how things had worked out, and spent most of the evening propped up by Dusk's sled, talking about pumas and Patagonia. Floyd accepted the food he was offered and sat alone by the fire, looking tired but for once not in pain. He went to bed as soon as the first cutter did; Jon followed him not long after. Iris was still eating, savoring the tender meat, when Lydia sat down beside her.

Iris glanced at her. "You knew about Jon's plan."

"Seems that way, doesn't it." She looked at Iris, taking her in, cataloguing her injuries. "You've been busy."

"Doesn't pay to be idle."

They were quiet for a while, although their silence was comfortable.

Lydia drank from a tall mug. When it was empty, she spoke again. "You're going all the way with him, then." Her head was tilted to the sky. "Patagonia."

"We are."

"Thought you liked it here."

"I like it a lot." Iris licked grease from her fingers. "But I'm not sure I fit in."

"What makes you think you'll fit in there?"

"I might not." Iris smiled. Pointed her chin over the fire at Dusk's sled. "But she will."

Lydia followed the line of her gaze. "I'm glad you didn't try to kill her. And I'm glad you're helping Jon." Then she turned back to Iris, her face serious. "But what will you do once you've released her?"

Iris fidgeted. She felt like she was being interrogated. "Jon's family has a farm. A few farms, I think. Says he'll have plenty of work for us."

Again they went quiet. It was Lydia who eventually broke the silence. "Well, I wish you luck."

Iris felt herself becoming frustrated. "You don't trust him?"

Lydia shrugged. "He seems a decent sort. Maybe more than decent." The same sad smile Iris had seen on her face the last time they spoke had reappeared. "I trust him about as much as I trust any of you."

"He's different. Patagonia will be different." Iris thought of what she'd overheard Jon telling Floyd. Of the great rivers, of the glaciers, of the guanaco—whatever a guanaco was. "Floyd and I need something different."

The fire spat. Lydia rubbed her eyes. "Can't be that different."

"How would you know?"

Lydia climbed to her feet. Laid a warm hand on Iris's shoulder, then walked away slowly, toward her house, speaking over her shoulder as she went.

"How do you reckon his family got their farms?"

16

THE CUTTERS WHEELED the finished cage out at dawn, parked it beside the sled, and invited Jon and the twins to inspect it. Iris knew little about carpentry, but it seemed sturdy enough to her. Then she remembered the speed at which Dusk had charged at her, the force with which the puma's body had hit her own. She tugged on the wooden bars, peered at the metal latches. Looked over at Dusk, at her twitching whiskers.

Jon seemed satisfied. He ran his hands over the cage's frame, clapped the cutters on the back, poured coins into their hands. He had one final request for them—to help move Dusk inside it. They cautiously obliged by sliding her body onto a large canvas sheet, angling some logs into the wagon door and hesitantly dragging the sheet up and into the cage. When that was done they closed the door and fastened the latch.

Floyd had been watching the cutters work, holding

himself stiffly. Iris could tell that he'd had a bad night, that he would have a bad day. But when Jon looked triumphantly at Floyd he grinned back, and she could see that his happiness was genuine. It was, she supposed, a significant achievement. With Dusk safely contained, they had done it: they had caught her.

Lydia came to them as the twins were hitching their horses to the wagon. She was holding a large bark parcel.

"Here," she said. "For when she wakes up."

Iris thanked her, took the bark from her hands and pulled back its top fold. Inside she saw dry ruby slabs of kangaroo meat.

She wanted to say more to Lydia. She wanted her to know that she knew Lydia was right, that perhaps there was no place for Iris anywhere, no untouched country where she could slide into the world's seams without causing harm—but that she was going to keep searching, that she would not stop searching. Yet she couldn't figure out how to get any of it out. Instead she just looked at her, and perhaps that was enough, because Lydia seemed to read some of it in her face.

She reached out. Touched Iris's elbow. "Might see you again."

Iris opened her mouth. Closed it. Nodded. "Might."

And then Lydia was walking away, and Jon had climbed onto the wagon's seat and started nickering at the horses, who had begun to walk down the path, and the wagon was trundling smoothly along behind them. Floyd had fallen into step with the horses, so Iris did, too.

Once more they followed the river, heading south toward yet another rocky range. The wagon carved ruts in the soft soil as the horses pulled it slowly along the bank. By mid-morning they'd reached the mountains and begun moving through a narrow gap. Its clear path and snowless forest was far easier to navigate than the one they'd passed through to reach Rossdale. Above them large birds cut and called through the wind: cockatoos, currawongs, high hawks. The river ran placid.

In the shadow of the peaks, Dusk woke up. Floyd was the first to realize. He slowed his stride, looking at her side-on. Iris noticed what he was doing, and then Jon did, too. They turned to the cage and saw the green-gold heat of Dusk's eyes studying them with intensity, even as she stayed prone.

The three of them glanced at each other. Dusk remained still. Then a growl began rumbling out of her: deep, loud, guttural.

Iris felt her heart quicken, felt her skin prickle and

chill. She moved to her horse, grabbed the bark package Lydia had given them, took out a slab of meat and carefully pushed it into the cage. The growling stopped. Dusk sniffed the meat. Her wide, pink tongue snaked out of her mouth and dragged across the dark flesh. Her great jaw levered open. As the wet smack of Dusk's feasting bounced off the rising rock, they continued through the pass.

On the other side of the mountains they found that the land had lost its lonely trees, its coat of bones. The plains had morphed from peat and buttongrass back into the ordered fields they'd seen early in their journey. The river flowed past fences, pastures, a wide uniformity of flat green grass.

Iris struggled to orient herself. She knew they were traveling back toward the rocky trail she and Floyd had climbed up when they'd arrived in the highlands, but they were approaching from a different direction. And there were so many plains, so many mountains; she couldn't figure out where they were in relation to where they had been, and she had no idea how far they were from their destination. She could have asked Jon—or Floyd, who probably had no doubt about where they were or how long this journey would take them—but her head was throbbing, and the idea of having something explained to her was tiring even to contemplate, so she stayed quiet.

She walked on, peering at the fields, until she saw something hulking in the distance, a large object, square-shaped and dusty yellow. She stared at it, then at the world around it—the distant forest, the shape of the peaks on the horizon—until she felt sure that this structure was what she thought it was: MacLaverty's homestead.

She glanced at Floyd. He had seen it, too. He was rubbing his back, but he was smiling. Iris realized how far they'd come, how close they were to the edge of the highlands. In a day and a half they'd arrive at the coast, perhaps sooner. Up on the seat of the wagon, Jon was whistling.

Moments after Iris recognized the homestead, Dusk rose to her feet and began padding about the cage, knocking over the pot of water they'd given her. She did not growl, but her long tail swished through the gaps in the timber. The muscles in her shoulders and haunches rolled beneath her fine fur, and each breath was like the bellows of a forge, and the glow of her eyes seemed to burn into Iris's skin.

In her pacing Dusk inspected each corner of the cage, but did not seem interested in escaping—not until she lifted a heavy paw and tapped it on one of the hinges.

The door gave a faint wobble. Dusk pulled her paw back, then slammed it into the hinge with shocking speed. The force, harder than the kick of a mule, shook the cage. Splinters flew from the site of her blow.

The horses stopped. Jon swung around on his seat. The twins froze. All of them stared at Dusk, who was watching the door shake on its hinge. Then she lay down again, as if bored, or satisfied she could tear the timber apart whenever she pleased.

Worried looks passed between the three of them, but there was little they could do, so they fed the puma another slab of meat and kept moving. Through the fenced fields they traveled, now seeing the odd bull, clusters of sheep, here and there a man watching the flocks. They raised their hands in greeting toward the shepherds but made no move toward them. They hadn't spoken of it, but they all knew how dangerous it would be to be discovered with Dusk alive in the wagon. There was no way of knowing how anyone would react, and every chance that word would spread.

They followed the river to where it ended: a large lake, ringed by hills. It was metal-gray, bordered by pink-white sand, with a calm, unrippled face. Iris was struck by how similar it was to the lake they'd seen on their first day in

the highlands, until she looked across the water and saw a
tall wooden building cradled by arcing alabaster columns.

Jon slowed the horses, pulled the wagon to a halt.
Gazed over at the Little Rest. "Wouldn't a bed be nice."

Floyd looked at Iris. "Be lovely." Humor in his expression. "If you reckon it's worth the trouble."

Jon looked over his shoulder. Dusk's huge eyes blinked
back at him. "No, I suppose not." He clicked his tongue at
the horses, who resumed walking. "We can camp on the
far shore. Tomorrow we'll make our descent."

They skirted around the lake, the late-afternoon sun
warming their cheeks and necks. They were calm, they
were tired and, for once, they weren't cold.

From the plain emerged a herd of deer, skipping into
view, down to the lake, dipping their heads to the water. A
stag was at their head, antlers silhouetted against the sky.
He watched the wagon approach while the does drank,
and when the space between horses and deer was under
a hundred yards he pulled his herd up and away. They
flew over rock and grass, their thin legs blurring, their collected bodies a smooth mass of fur. Dusk watched them,
but did not react.

And perhaps it was once again seeing these fleet, curious
creatures; or perhaps it was the sight of the Little Rest and
its cradle of bones; or the knowledge of how soon they'd
leave; or the closeness of the unmoving water—whatever
it was, Iris began to feel the loss of these highlands aching

through her, even though she hadn't quite left them behind. She did not regret the choice to take Dusk home. It was just that she could feel the land ebbing out of her, and with each pulse of peak and plain she felt like she was losing something she would never get back.

They did not speak much through the final part of the day. Eventually they stopped at a gentle cove in the lake, beside a windbreak of gnarled, gray-white trees. Sunset was under an hour away, so they hurried about gathering firewood, brushing down horses, collecting water, putting up tents. They were so busy that they didn't notice what was happening in the middle distance, and then the near.

It was Dusk who first became aware of it. A deep growl shuddered out of her jaws and around the campsite, far louder than it had been earlier in the day. They paused their tasks to look at her, and saw that she was standing up, hackles raised. She wasn't pacing or trying to escape—she was standing still, facing the beach. When Iris realized that Dusk wasn't about to smash through the cage she turned in the direction the puma was facing and saw the group of riders, galloping toward them.

At first she thought they might be fellow travelers. Then she noted how fast they were coming, how hard they were beating their horses. She turned to Floyd, but he was already moving. Their own horses had been drinking from the lake, and he was dragging them by their bridles back toward the wagon, trying to hitch them as fast as he could. Jon was standing, watching the rapidly approaching group.

Iris gathered their saddlebags as Floyd began turning the wagon around. He had it facing the trail when the riders arrived.

There were a dozen of them, and at their head were Lyle Horton and Harriet MacLaverty. Behind them were a few well-dressed, gentlemanly sort of folk—other graziers, Iris assumed. With them were a few shabbier sorts, perhaps their servants or workers they'd hired. Then Iris saw the figure trailing at their rear, riding slower than the rest, sitting slanted in his saddle. A tall figure. Broad-backed, lightly bearded. A familiar little smile playing on his lips.

Her first instinct was to scream, not with fear but with rage, the wild rage of a storm. She felt for the knife at her belt, she looked around for a heavy rock, she tasted copper in the burning of her throat. She calculated how long it would take to reach him. She tried to make sense of his survival, but she couldn't concentrate, couldn't focus on anything other than her fury, and the dread that was crawling in beside it, twisting her stomach, icing her blood.

The horses came to a halt and their riders dismounted. Patrick Lees was close enough now for her to see him more clearly, and her rage and horror suddenly abated. He had changed since their last encounter, most obviously in his right leg, which swung behind the rest of his body in a stiff limp. The entire right side of him was slack, she saw, the flesh dragging heavily down his frame. His right arm flopped uselessly by his side. His right eye was a glazed ball. Even the hair on that side of his scalp looked flaccid and lifeless, and his small, smug smile was only present in the half of his mouth that could manage it. The other side hung loose and numb.

He opened his mouth as if to speak, but nothing came out. It occurred to Iris that he no longer could, and even in the red vortex of her rage she felt a pulse of pleasure. She began gathering saliva to spit at him, but was interrupted by Dusk, who had started hissing, yowling, displaying the vast armory of her teeth. Iris glanced at her, and saw how she had unsheathed her claws and was slashing them across the cage's bars.

Jon began walking toward the group. Iris considered taking out her knife and running past him, but then she remembered Floyd. She looked over to him and in his eyes found not anger, but grim despair. He too had seen Lees, yet was focusing on Iris, and on the racket Dusk was making. He moved to position himself in front of his sister, as if he'd read her intentions.

Iris felt an urge to copy Dusk. To show her teeth, to show Patrick Lees the fullness of her wide, wounded smile.

Lyle Horton was striding toward the wagon. His cream suit was spattered with mud, his beard and mustache were shaking, and he was pointing a hand at all three of them. "You whoreson liars. You fucking thieves."

Jon stopped, raised his palms. "Nobody has lied to you, Mr. Horton. And nobody has stolen anything." He pointed at Patrick Lees. "At least, we haven't. Surely you can recognize my rifle on your companion's back."

Half of Lees' face curled into a sneer, and a wordless grunt slithered out of his lips. Iris remembered what he'd said to her when she'd last seen him, and she was burning again, her vision flashing with blood and blades and fire. She felt woozy; she felt drained.

Horton continued, his voice rising. "Oh, he's told us what you did to him. How you betrayed him after he led you to the beast's lair. How you tortured him with your poisons. How you planned on robbing us of our justice so you could sell this monster in your homeland for a fortune. You never thought we'd find that out, did you? The young man here knew you'd try to sneak away if you got your hands on her, so he came straight to us." He shifted his outstretched hand in Lees' direction. "He had to write it all down with his left hand. If only you were half as brave as he is."

"That's beyond a lie. This foul—"

"Shut your mouth!" Horton was bellowing now, red-faced and trembling.

At the rising of his voice Dusk released an unholy, piercing scream. Everyone leaped, and she renewed her attack on the cage, hurling her shoulder into the door, banging and crashing at its bindings. The wagon began rocking on its wheels. Small chunks of wood were flying off its frame.

Jon's eyes were flashing between Horton and Lees, outrage all over his face.

Floyd moved to his side. "Jon." Laid a hand on his shoulder, began walking him out of the way, back toward their horses. "There's no use."

Horton blinked at Floyd, and the anger in his voice turned bitter. "And to think I trusted you! What a fool I was." He turned his glare to Iris. "Scum is scum. Nothing changes."

Dusk was panting between her screams. She had stopped crashing into the cage with her bulk and was now set on destroying it with her dextrous claws. A large wooden bar snapped under one of her blows, and one of her front limbs thrashed out of it, tearing vicious arcs through the air.

As she did this Harriet MacLaverty came forward, focusing not on the men, but on Iris.

"I don't know what he's told you, but please, step away from the cage." Gentle reason in her voice. "This has to be done. She's too dangerous to live. And I'll still pay you."

"Like hell!" roared Horton. "You'll be lucky if we don't string the three of you up."

MacLaverty ignored him. "It'll be all right, I promise." She was trying to be placid, soothing, but disappointment was etched on her face. "What were you thinking?"

Iris stepped back, up against the lurching cage, just out of reach of Dusk's swinging claws. Horton was gesturing at Patrick Lees. "Give me that rifle."

Lees stumbled forward, ugly satisfaction on his collapsed face. Horton snatched the gun from him, inspected its chamber. "Shot. Get me some powder and goddamn shot."

One of his men scurried back to their horses. Another fished through his pockets.

Floyd had moved Jon over to the horses but Jon was still talking to the graziers, pleading with them to stop, saying that Dusk was no danger to them, that he'd take her away and they wouldn't need to spend a penny. Horton, waiting impatiently, was telling him to shut his foreign mouth.

Iris was wobbling on her feet. Her rage was shrinking, and awareness of the situation threatened to overwhelm her. Despair overrode her thoughts; panic pushed at her instincts. She became aware of Dusk's savagery doubling behind her. Felt the storm of splinters falling into her hair. She reached out to the cage to steady herself, grasping a piece of metal that was pleasantly, calmingly cold.

Horton received his ammunition and tried to tumble it into the rifle, but dropped it on the ground. As the grazier bent to pick it up, Floyd turned to Iris and came toward her, seemingly to be nearer to her. Then he looked at her more closely.

His eyes, so expert in the art of noticing, went wide. Suddenly he laughed. He was clutching the base of his back, and he was obviously so stiff, so sore, and everything had come to nothing for them, Iris thought, perhaps their whole lives—everything broken, everything ruined.

But Floyd's laughter was genuine, she realized. And then he was walking backward, to the front of the wagon, and unhitching the horses. Uncomprehending, she glanced down to where his eyes had been fixed, on her hand, and she saw it—the piece of metal in her palm was the latch of the wagon's door.

*

Dusk's fury was crashing into Iris's ears like a falling river. She looked to their horses, now standing free. Floyd was fastening their saddlebags and muttering rapidly to Jon, whose face was shifting with understanding.

The sun was low now, cutting into the horizon.

As Horton fiddled with his shot, and the other riders waited by the lake, uncertain of their next move, Iris saw how things might go. How she might, although it was unlikely, make it to the horses in time. How they might just be able to carry three injured people. She saw how their horses would gallop, tenacious and loyal, all the way to the rocky passage. She saw how the three of them would dismount and scramble down the path, how they would crash along toward the coast, how they would board a great ship. How she and Floyd would cross a mountainous ocean as their parents had done decades earlier, bound not for harsh imprisonment but for rough freedom. She saw how she would taste the salted air; how she would witness the beasts that lived in the waves, terrible and beautiful, with ribs like trees, torsos the size of taverns, jaws as wide as caves. She saw herself watching them from the rolling deck, before closing her eyes and waiting to be delivered to a distant shore, wild and strange, a land they didn't know, full of people who didn't know them. A place of fresh dreams and new troubles: of new names.

*

Dusk was kicking with her back legs now, which were even stronger than her forelimbs. Nails were popping out of the frame.

Iris looked at the riders by the lake. She lifted her eyes above Horton's fumbling rifle, above Patrick Lees' lopsided malice. She gazed at the snowy peaks, at the shine of the lake, at the uncountable colors of the tarns and grasses and trees, their mirrored worlds and varied textures, stretching to the rocky horizon. The dark shapes of birds, littering the high air. The ghostly ribs surrounding the inn.

The latch was cold and heavy as she tightened her grip. Dusk stopped kicking, and Iris felt the puma shudder with power as she lowered herself into a crouch, as if she knew what was about to happen.

The graziers had finally noticed Iris's hand and were scrabbling for their weapons. One of the men was yelling.

Iris let the sound of them wash over her like weak rain. She closed her eyes, she tasted the clean air, she summoned into her mind the endless light of the highland stars. Then she stepped to the side, lifted the latch, and ripped the cage door open.

Acknowledgments

My boundless thanks to: David Winter, Peter Straus, Geordie Williamson, Praveen Naidoo, Bri Collins, Dave Cain, Tom Evans, Richard and Majda Flanagan, Stephen Edwards, Clara Farmer, Eugenia Dubini, Eva-Marie von Hippel, Emily Bill, Esther Arnott and Bonorong Wildlife Sanctuary.